THE DREAM QUEST

BY DON PARESI

NORTHERN ICE
NORTH
AND
SOUTH
AMERICA
MANY YEARS AFTER
THE OLD WAR
ARPOCH
SAINTS DAGGER
THE VOYAGE
OF
THE KELLA
AVANEX
ISLE
OF THE
GOLD MAN
ARCHELAPAGO OF
VALAGUENA
XOTH
N
REALM OF THE OLD GODS

Keisha stood against the view screen of the ship with the great dome of the sky as her backdrop. To Kastos she appeared almost primal, as if she were not human, just an animal inside of a human shell. Her eyes were feral, almost hostile. Kastos decided to tread carefully around her, not wanting to become vexed, or worse.

"I can't thank you enough for your help," Kastos offered, then held his arms out to the wild-looking female.

"We will continue on our journey to the shore of the old gods now," Keisha said.

Kastos looked at the compass. The ship was drifting on uncharted waters.

"How are we supposed to get there now without a crew?" Kastos said, giving her a baleful glance. "And without a navigator, how shall we even find it? Reech is gone."

"Take these," she said, holding out the bracelets towards him, "with these the ship will obey your every command."

Kastos wondered if this was a trick, if he would turn into a fish-man if he accepted them, but intuition told him that it was right for him to have them. So, without hesitating, he clasped them on to both of his arms, for better or worse.

ISBN 978-1-949914-65-8

For information address Crossroad Press at 141 Brayden Dr., Hertford, NC 27944
A Mystique Press Production -Mystique Press is an imprint of Crossroad Press.
www.crossroadpress.com

First edition

1

The tandem suns sailing above the great western ocean painted the horizon with a beautiful wash of blue and gold. The waters of the bottomless sea were on fire from their twin reflections, giving the coastland city of Arpoch entirely more credit than it was due. After the old wars, all that remained of the municipality had never been rebuilt. Instead it had been left to crumble into the sandstone that it had been reared upon. However, in the colorful light of the double stars even this dead port had a strange kind of beauty.

Some of the structures down by the rusted-out oceanfront were partially still intact, and surprisingly there was even a working pier. However, most of the other buildings had long been abandoned.

From the shadows of three unused, towering refinery storage bins, a man emerged wearing a grey hooded sweatshirt. Dressed warm for the bitter, windy weather in what used to be known as the month of March, he appeared to have hiked from wherever it was that he came from. On his shoulders he carried a very worn-out looking backpack, a bedroll and an old, beat-up, yet reliable, Browning rifle.

In one hand he held a piece of scrolled pemmican that contained a message that was written in black sap. Now that computers, pens and papers were a thing of the past, other means for writing had to be utilized. He had found it outside of his hut in the Yukon Wastes nailed to an old tree. It was a note that advertised employment on a sea voyage for some honest, working men—something that was near impossible to find these days in a world filled with thieves, cannibals and other horrors best not described.

Arpoch had been rampant with mutant creatures until after the western republic had cleared them out. Then the city had been set up as a base, and its ships had been rebuilt and converted into sail-and-steam vessels. Since the gunnery had been run mostly by computers before the great loss of power, the small arms were all that were still useful. Ammunition for them was manufactured in small "mom and pop" style gun mills that had sprouted up everywhere as a marketable business in the end days.

The lone walking man had an unusual stride, for every few yards he would stop and stretch his arms into the air, for no apparent reason. Perhaps he was trying to crack his back, or open up his respiratory system. It was a peculiar gait, one that had earned him the name "Reech."

Reech was roughly about fifty-four years old, which made him an unlikely candidate for a crewmember, especially with his strange walk. However, Reech had the navigational skills needed to read the charts and instruments that would guide the ship. If no one else came to claim the position already, then Reech had a job. Not only was Reech skilled in the reading of maps, but he had an uncanny knack that could help him guide vessels through uncharted waters with no help from any instruments.

Another few steps and the slow walker passed the great coal bins that were filled with fuel for the boats. Everything in Arpoch had been converted over to steam power. Coal was easy enough to obtain by mining, but wood was difficult to find, any that burned well anyhow. All of the forests surrounding Arpoch had been long scourged and laid to waste by weapons of mass destruction. It was all contaminated ash.

Once through the storage yard, Reech entered the docks, and in the spectacular light of the twin, sinking oval suns he finally saw the moored *Kella*.

Once upon a time it may have worn a haze-gray military coat of paint, but here was a colorful floating mural of graphic design. On it were finely rendered depictions of fantastical ocean creatures, coral reefs and palm trees. He smiled at the large sharks' teeth painted on the bow. The name "Kella" was put in large, stylized script just above them.

He hiked his sagging, old backpack higher and looked up at the single stack centered upon the superstructure. The twin suns had already descended behind it and blinded his vision so that he couldn't see if any men were posted on the frigate's quarterdeck.

Hesitantly, he placed one hand upon the handrail and walked up the gangplank of the ship.

On the signal deck, where he watched from his shack on high, a small brown pygmy man known as Gank, with a round, protruding belly dressed in shorts, spotted the man with the strange step as he came up to the quarterdeck. A sense of urgency hit him and he realized all too late that he had missed seeing the man arrive from a distance because he had fallen asleep.

"Fuck!" Gank extorted, as he swung his feet down from where he had been resting, jumped up from the steel folding chair he sat on, and ran with the strange agility that only small, fat people seem to possess. He reached a ladder that brought him down to the main weather deck and disappeared into a hatchway that led into the confines of the ship.

In doing so he had failed to notice the tiny boat that came up to the starboard side and the man who climbed out clad in a black cape and a stylish hat. Then, similar to a silent ninja warrior, the man crawled up the side of the *Kella*'s hull, by using strange gloves that had the ability to cling to the vessel's side.

Once on board, the stranger found an open hatch in the garishly painted bulkhead and made his way into the belly of the ship.

Reech finally made it to the quarterdeck where he met two men standing sentry duty. There was no salute or formality, because this was a private vessel. Reech handed over the scroll of skin with the writing on it to the closest guard. He was a big man with a full beard and extremely hairy hands, and many tattoos of a very poor quality on his forearm. The other was an older gentleman with no hair left who looked even more worn and torn than Reech. Both of these men were dressed in army uniforms, regardless of the fact that they were on board an old navy frigate.

"You are looking for employment aboard this ship?" the larger man asked, and his eyes glittered with a mischievous look that made Reech feel uncomfortable. He also felt his hackles rise slightly when he saw the holstered pistol that the big man carried.

"Yes," Reech answered, "I have traveled very far, all the way down from the Yukon Wastes."

The large man grunted while he lowered his head to read the script, and the old man next to him took a swig from something in a leather flask. When the older chap let out a belch that stank like dead rats mixed with pine cleaner, it made Reech actually wrinkle his nose.

The sentries obviously didn't appear to be concerned with sobriety while on watch. Something else that left Reech feeling that it was a suspicious situation.

"The captain isn't here to receive any new crewmembers right now. If you'd like, you can wait in the seaman division until he comes back. Go down one deck and then follow the passageway up to the bow. You'll see the hatchway … and leave your weapon here."

Reech didn't like it, but it was a long walk back to the Yukon Wastes, so he had little choice but to comply. He placed the Browning against the podium with an air of heavy reluctance.

"Don't worry," the big man assured, "you can have it back once you're signed in by the captain … or if you leave."

Reech shrugged, then walked by the two watchmen and entered the ship's interior. As he did so, he failed to notice the wide grin that spread over the larger guard's face.

Belowdecks in the cramped compartment of the seaman division, a tall, lanky man called Turkeyneck was looking through the hatchway at the approaching, odd-walking Reech.

"Here he comes," he warned.

Quickly, Turkeyneck stepped back and allowed the larger sailors holding the ropes to come forward. The two big men were giggling like schoolgirls as they readied themselves to carry out the traditional hazing of the new guy.

"Man did you see the way he walks, stopping to stretch every ten steps … is Kastos serious?" Turkeyneck hissed at the men as they waited. Some of them were still laughing it up.

"Do you guys wanna shut the fuck up before he hears you?" Buckshot said, a mean-tempered boatswain's mate, who then reached with a large, meaty hand and slapped Turkeyneck in the head, who in turn verbally retaliated by calling the woodsman an asshole. Then the metal hatch door began to slowly creak open as the new member of the *Kella* stepped into the dark compartment.

"GET HIM!" Turkeyneck yelled as Reech swung the door open wide in order to allow himself into the trap.

Abruptly the compartment filled with the sound of shouting and scuffling, and in a matter of two seconds, Reech had been subdued. He reacted with a viper's quickness, giving a good account of himself that was surprising for a man who looked as aged as shoe leather and managed to plant a punch on the first man who grabbed him. He hit his opponent square in the face, which squashed his nose and even knocked him back a few steps. However, the second brute came over and clutched Reech in a half nelson that rendered him inert, keeping him down as Turkeyneck and the others moved in with the ropes. Moments later, the cotton-haired joe was laid out like a trussed-up hog ready for the slaughter.

Turkeyneck nodded with satisfaction, which gave the signal to one of his cohorts to proceed with the next event, which was to strip down the victim and tar and feather his naked buttocks. Next came a fat fellow with a face rampant with scars, brandishing the pitch-covered paintbrush and bucket filled with tar, all set to apply the sticky coating before Turkeyneck could dump on the feathers. Reech continued to thrash and protest, although it was in vain. Between the muscles on the gang of hazers and the knots in the ropes, he had been overcome.

Suddenly the hatchway opened, unattended as it was due to the busy task of the melee, and in jumped a slim, dapper stranger dressed in a long black cape. It draped behind him like the folded wings of a dragon and on his head he wore a wide-brimmed, jaunty hat adorned with a scarlet feather. His eyes were a piercing cold-gray color, and his face was wolfishly handsome, complete with a thin mustache and beard that gave him a dashing appearance. In his hand he held a saber with a bejeweled hilt that was probably worth more than the entire crew and the *Kella* alike.

"Hey now," the swordsman said. "That's no way to treat a navigator. I say untie him at once or taste some steel, you filthy, dirt-caked bags of shit."

Everyone stopped at once. All eyes were on the man standing at the door, staring at him as if he were a ghost.

It was Turkeyneck who was the first to break out of the lull caused by this unexpected visitor. His face twisted into a scowl of contempt, then broadened into a huge grin, showing off all four of his teeth that were dirt-black with chewing tobacco. He sauntered up to the man in the slick outfit, and pulled a long scaling knife out of his waist band. Then Turkeyneck made the fatal mistake of pointing it at the stranger and applying pressure with the point of it against his chest.

"What if I tell you to go and find a nice place to jump off this boat before we …"

Turkeyneck never had a chance to finish his sentence. The bearded interloper ran his sword through him with a speed that was unmatched by anything anyone on board the ship had ever seen. Turkeyneck took on a terrible look of shock and then collapsed into a heap, a pool of blood spreading out from beneath him and also from his tobacco-stuffed mouth.

The swordsman then took a rag from his own pocket to wipe the blade clean, a look of disdain on his face as if perhaps he was thinking that the hazer's plasma was contaminated.

"Anyone else like to try to tar and feather my ward? Be my guest. Nobody fucks with Reech but *me*, got it?" Then he slid the sword with the bejeweled hilt back into its scabbard with amazing speed, as if to remind everyone that the hand is indeed quicker than the eye.

"You … you fucking killed Turkeyneck," the hazer who held the bucket of tar in his hands said. "GOOD!" After placing the container down on the floor, the plump man took out his boatswain's knife and commenced to cut Reech's bindings loose. "He was an *asshole* anyway … this was all his doing … right, everybody?"

Everyone in the compartment nodded and muttered in agreement, none of them fighting men, or offering up any challenges. In fact, the two bigger men began to pick up Turkeyneck's carcass and then carried him topside to throw him to the sharks. Since Arpoch was a deserted base, there was no one to worry about seeing them. "Good riddance to the shit monkey," and other charming epithets seemed to be the common phrase among them. Then the man with the cape and sword pulled up a battered blue plastic chair, sat down and propped his booted feet on the table. He kept a watchful eye on everyone as they restored the room to a relatively normal setting. Reech was escorted to sit in another blighted seat next to the swordsman, and given a drink of water and a number of apologies, all of which he welcomed with wafer-thin appreciation.

2

At last the pygmy came to the door marked CAPTAIN'S QUARTERS in engraved letters on a mounted brass plate. It had long gone green like all of the rest of the brass fittings on board ship, since there was no longer anything left to polish it with. Gank stared nervously at the oaken barrier between him and the madman that he had worked under for the past ten years, and wondered what his reaction would be upon being disturbed.

Above him were two glowing plankton globes made from the skins of mutated blowfish. Each had several pairs of odd eyes and fins, and one even had a second head. A result of the radiation no doubt, all of which had pretty much dissipated after the old wars, except for a few hot spots here and there. So even after an age and a half the lower strains of sea life were still suffering genetic disorders. Gank had a thought that perhaps most of the people he knew on board this vessel were just a short throw from the same affliction as well.

With a heavy feeling upon his chest the short black man rapped solidly on the private chamber of the captain. At first there was no answer, then in a low, nearly inaudible voice Gank heard a "come in" emanate from behind the door.

Gank opened it and stepped into the dimly candlelit quarters of Kastos the high adventurer. The captain preferred the traditional way to light a room rather than using microscopic creatures trapped inside of an inflated fish. Once Gank's vision had adjusted to the darkness he was able to see the interior of the chamber, and his fearless leader.

"My Captain," Gank announced as he entered, feeling the need to present his case almost immediately, as if he might be reprimanded for the trespass if he did not express good reason. Yet once inside, he stopped himself short.

Everywhere Gank looked he saw mountains of clutter. Mostly books, charts and maps more than anything. These filled every nook and cranny of the room. There were also special mahogany shelves worked into the walls where more books, scrolls and skin parchments were stored. These flanked a large porthole that was curtained, barely exhibiting the final light of the setting tandem suns seeping in.

Below the window stood a large wooden table with a map unfurled upon it, along with several measuring instruments and devices, mostly calipers, sextants and other tools needed for navigation. Seated behind this table in an ill-matched old, worn office leather cushion chair was Kastos the high adventurer. He was a large man, almost seven feet tall, broad shouldered with toned, muscular arms and a fighting man's girth. He was dressed in an old army field uniform with the sleeves cut off to show off his gunboat-size limbs, along with a pair of fatigue pants that were tucked into combat boots. His hair was long, straight and red in color and he had a trim beard and mustache of a slightly darker hue. His teeth were white and straight, which was a miracle in these apocalyptic wastelands where most people had trench mouth disease. His piercing, black eyes were now glazed and red from poring over the papers that were spread all over his desk, and by the looks of the candlestick stubs it was evident that Kastos had been at it all day.

"Captain Kastos ... *sir!*"

Kastos looked up at the pygmy dreamily and his mouth dropped open as if he were about to yawn. He appeared exhausted.

"Gank," Kastos uttered in a garbled voice, having not spoken to anyone all day, so now his unused voice box sounded a little rusty. "What is it, man?"

The midget gave the customary salute which Kastos disregarded, instead waving him on to speak. A look of urgency was in the messenger's eyes, so Kastos became alert.

"It's the navigator, sir," Gank rubbed his small brown hands together nervously, "he has arrived, he is on board ship, sir."

It was almost as if the candles on the wooden table flared towards the large, gray overhead angle-irons for a second, but it was really Kastos' eyes and his demeanor that had brightened. At the sound of the news the captain cheered, then pushed back his chair and stood up. He then held out his arms and showed Gank all the work he had done so far in plotting their course.

"I have worked out the coordinates of our heading, and I have to say that it makes absolutely no sense to me how to find something that is not on any map. I have gone over these maps and charts until my head is pounding like a blacksmith's hammer upon the anvil. And I still only know how to take us to the threshold of the forbidden realm … I have no clue what lies beyond. Now if what you tell me is true and this so-called special-case quartermaster is here … then we will be celebrating, my lad!"

Kastos took a huge earthen jug filled with stone liquor, pulled the cork and swallowed a huge draught. After a hearty belch he then handed it to Gank, evidently expecting the messenger to do the same. The pygmy grasped the container, sniffed the contents, pretended to take a sip and then placed the jug back on the table.

"I'll go fetch him for you, sir," Gank invited, "I believe he went below decks."

"All right, go then and make it quick," Kastos ordered him off with a curt salute, and then opened the porthole to let in some of the sea air. Gank turned to leave and reached out for the door handle when suddenly another knock sounded from its outer side.

Gank looked towards Kastos, who was finishing off another shot of cheer. "Open it," Kastos said through a tightly strained voice.

It was Reech, and standing behind him was the man in the black swordfighter's garb, complete with a cape and jaunty hat. Kastos took measure of him and instantly assumed that he was the older man's fighting escort. He regarded the both of them with raised eyebrows.

"Greetings Captain Kastos, I am Reech," the older man said, "I am here for the navigator position. Word has come to me in the far north that you seek a quartermaster."

He walked into the room at an odd pace; every few feet he would stop in order to stretch his hands up above his head as if to crack his back. Then he held out a calloused, overly large and knobby hand to shake with Kastos.

The captain took it and then allowed Reech to examine the mess on his table, where he had wasted the entire day trying to make sense out of a course that needed proper plotting.

"It's all yours, champ," he said. "See if you can figure out a way to find the way to the shores where the old gods supposedly exist."

The dandy-looking dude in the black Zorro attire bowed before Kastos and then removed his wide-brimmed, red-feathered hat, letting his straight black hair fall out. Kastos liked him immediately, feeling a kindred spirit in the way this man grew his hair ... like the fabled rock musicians from before the old wars.

"My name is Trantos," the swordsman introduced himself. "I hail originally from a far-off land across the wasted continent in a town known as Lyseum, where Reech and I were old friends. He had come to live in the Yukon Wastes, but sent word for me to meet him here ... he spoke of a voyage to a mysterious place."

Kastos raised his eyebrows in curiosity. He had heard that the eastern shore was a mutant wasteland filled with death. It was quartered off and labeled the Exclusion Zone.

"Really, I had heard that nobody existed beyond the desert. I guess you must be living proof that I have been misinformed." Kastos replied.

Trantos placed his hat back onto his head and smiled. "There is some truth to those tales. The eastern seaboard is quite treacherous; only in the green veldt of the northeast would you find a very small inhabited province."

Kastos noticed that Gank was still standing by the door.

"Did you want another shot?"

The pygmy jumped as if he were just pinched.

"What? Oh no, sir, I'm fine, I'm leaving now."

Kastos grinned as the mini-man gingerly closed the oak door behind him so as not to make a sound. Only the tiny click of the old latch gripping the inset within the frame was heard.

"So," Kastos went on, "you have come all that way?"

"I wish to come on the sea voyage." Trantos pronounced.

Both of them glanced over at Reech, who was sifting through maps and charts with a stern, owlish look upon his face.

"Well, since you have traveled so far across a ragged country with your comrade, I don't doubt that he told you about where we are going."

Trantos shook his head and shrugged.

"I am seeking the lost shore of the old gods, the continent of Xoth," Kastos informed Trantos. "Have you ever heard of it?"

The swordsman's eyes became dark, as if the name of the place gave him a chill.

"It's an old legend. I have heard that it's a very bad place."

Reech looked up from the table momentarily. His face appeared grave.

"Indeed," the old, gray-haired navigator said, "it is a fearful destination."

"Why do you want to go there?" Trantos asked.

Kastos spun away from the swordsman momentarily, lowered his head and leaned against the bulkhead on one outstretched arm.

"I have been haunted by a face in my dreams, a woman whom I cannot identify, but she tells me to find her in that place where I shall live forever ... I believe her, enough to pay any and all quite handsomely to help me reach that lost shore. Once there, everyone is to stay on the ship and leave immediately after dropping me off. I shall not return. I am to remain behind, because that is where I will find my destiny."

A moment of uneasy silence filled the room, as if no one knew how to respond to such a ludicrous notion.

"Yes," Trantos agreed, "dreams can have a significant meaning."

Kastos met his gaze and saw a strong sincerity in his eyes, as if he too had once before experienced the same siren song.

"I will sail with you to this place," Trantos stated, "and I will help you with your quest ... if you will have me. But first there is an issue to discuss. We had an incident below decks and unfortunately ... I killed one of your men."

Kastos looked at the sword wielder, honestly speechless over what he had just heard him confess.

The twin suns finally winked out below the line of the iridescent-colored sea, leaving the star constellations to take over their shift, as the lords of the night sky revealed their glittering stars. The crew began to settle in for the night. Kastos announced over the sound-powered intercom system that the ship would sail at dawn, so that meant wake-up time would be at least an hour beforehand. No cards or role-playing games allowed after lights out, nor even any unplugged music jams down in the storage hold. Normally the ship's bar would be open, but even that had been shut down. No drinking of stone liquor the day before getting underway unless you were Captain Kastos within his own private quarters and had your own stash.

Above the waters the mutant seagulls made their final feeding for the evening and headed to roost. There was not a single bird that did not suffer the degenerative effects of contamination. Many of them sported multiple sets of eyes or an extra foot, and some even had an extra wing growing out of their bellies, which caused them to flop clumsily throughout the sky. Normally Gank and one of his buddies would be seen standing on the railing outside of the signal shack smoking tobacco and laughing at the absurd creatures, but tonight only the hull technician known as Hairybear came out. The big man with the cheap tattoos who had welcomed Reech aboard strolled along the deck by himself, after finishing his watch on the quarterdeck. He liked to gaze into the sea at night when it was illuminated by the hoary, pitted face of the war-battered moon. Hairybear intended to watch only for a short time, then to retire and rest up for the unmooring at dawn.

Hairybear preferred to spend as much time away from the rest of the crew as he could in order to reflect on the good old days. Now he looked down at the water at his haggard reflection and sighed. Too many years had gone by in these wasted lands. He would be happy to leave these shores and find somewhere that had something left besides mutant rats and glowing hillsides. Still, he had to take a moment to revel in the hazing plan that he had set up for the new arrival. Hairybear chortled over the peculiar gait that the old guy displayed. Walking every two, three steps and then stopping to stretch towards the sky, as if perhaps trying to pop his spine back into place. Once Hairybear had spotted him he had told Turkeyneck to prepare the tar and feathers.

Hairybear couldn't wait to go below and hear about the initiation and see the new recruit. His reflection in the moonlit water was smiling, because now he was well satisfied that the dirty deed had been done. It always made him happy when he caused others misery.

Just then a horrible face emerged from below the surface of the water, right where Hairybear's reflection sat. It was the corpse of Turkeyneck, all bloated and covered with *bite marks.* The body arched its back and then cruised backwards, as if it were repelled by something.

Hairybear's mouth fell open as he beheld the gash on Turkeyneck's chest where he'd been stabbed. Evidently the hazing event had gone awry if his prime henchman had been pierced and then thrown to the lampreys.

Suddenly a great yellow shark, with two heads—one massive, the other slighter, yet equally as toothy—rose from the deep and nearly swallowed Turkeyneck whole. It closed its larger maw over the cadaver's head down to his shoulders and abruptly pulled him under the water. Then, as if showing off its great bulk and back fin in a farewell wave, it disappeared back into the depths with its prize. Hairybear was stunned beyond measure as his hands gripped onto the metal rail of the ship, so tightly that his knuckles were pure white.

After being dismissed and relieved from having to drink any more stone liquor, Gank descended into the berthing hold and found a spiffy seaman division compartment that even smelled like pine cleaner. He looked at the men making ready to bunk down and asked, "What's up?"

"We have an issue," Cosmo, a spaced-out looking vet with the fabled thousand-yard stare, came forward and said. "There was a stranger, he killed Turkeyneck ... we had to throw him overboard."

Gank went bug-eyed over this news, yet at the same time Cosmo could sense that he too felt no remorse. Nobody really cared much for Turkeyneck to begin with. All present could say that they had unfavorable experiences with him, and most of these merchant mariners had wanted to be rid of him from the first time they ever met him.

"Shouldn't we tell the captain?" Cosmo asked.

Gank thought it over. He didn't want this whole party of people going up and telling Kastos, it would be a better idea to keep everyone here. Besides, Gank had already just seen the stranger that Cosmo was talking about in the captain's quarters, and could guess that the captain already knew.

"I'll go and tell him."

The pygmy man walked over to the door, yet before he could even place his palm on the handle, it swung up, releasing the pressure so that it opened before he could touch it.

There stood Hairybear, big as life and twice as nasty with a face as red as a beet, looking as if he were ready to kill somebody.

Meanwhile, back in the captain's quarters, Kastos tried to reason things out for Trantos, "I must admit I appreciate your confession and turning yourself in, but this must be a situation most certainly brought on by some provocation!"

"A crime is indeed a crime!" Trantos held out his hands to be cuffed. Kastos wouldn't have it. He was certain that there was some justification for the killing that had yet to be discovered.

Kastos had consumed a good fill of stone liquor by now and was feeling the effects. He swayed back and forth as if the ship were already on the high seas. Trantos, who was also indulging in the drink, felt as if his legs were rubber, and he nearly spun out when suddenly a loud rapping at the door brought the both of them around to face it. Even Reech, who still had his nose in the maps and charts, looked up as the banging on the door escalated to a level that caused the ceramic bric-a-brac hanging on the nearby wall to come crashing to the floor.

"Who the hell," Kastos bellowed, taking on a fighting stance, and then Trantos pulled out his sword with a flash of steel. Another moment later and the door crashed open. It was Hairybear himself, who stood there with Gank the pygmy in tow. Hairybear reached around and yanked the meatball-shaped man forward, then pushed the door open. It swung back on him, almost comically. He bulled his way through it again, with one hand wrapped around Gank's neck, and the other placed threateningly on the butt of his gun. Then into the chamber he went as if the steel Trantos held was nothing more than an incidental threat that bore no danger.

"THIS MAN IS GUILTY OF KILLING A CREWMEMBER!" Hairybear shouted, then pointed over at the swordsman. Reech had both of his hands up, standing stiffly against the bulkhead as if a weapon had been drawn on him—which it hadn't, so he looked absurd. Trantos turned around quickly and his black cape whirled behind him in a flamboyant fashion as he spoke.

"Your welcoming commitee was ready to tar and feather the ship's navigator. I merely intervened by offering a choice: either stand down or face the wrath of my steel. The one called Turkeyneck decided the latter. I gave him fair quarter."

Hairybear gave Trantos a scowl, then gave the captain a hoary glance, clearly outraged over the fact that the Kastos was milling about with these two outlanders. Now one of his own had been slain and it looked as if nothing would be done about it. He also noticed that the captain was giving the dark, piercing hate glance towards him, the one recognized as his death gaze. Kastos no longer held the face of a man who had been drinking; instead he appeared as a sober sheriff ready to take on a bank robber, his hand rested upon the handle of his own pistol.

"Unhand my messenger now!" Kastos commanded.

Hairybear released his grip on Gank, who trotted behind the safety of the captain.

"Sorry, sir," the pygmy said, "I tried to keep it all under wraps, but Hairybear came into the compartment and rousted everyone out of bed and made them all spill the beans."

Kastos ignored the little brown man and continued to lock eyes with the man who had tried to haze his navigator without authorization.

"You want to take your hand off your weapon right now,

Hairybear, or we're gonna see which one of us wakes up in hell first tomorrow morning."

Hairybear hesitated, but then something in the captain's eyes made him feel unsure of himself. He had never seen anyone quicker on the draw than Kastos. That was why he was the captain of his own ship, not because he had been appointed.

Hairybear relented and dropped his hand from his gun.

"With all due respect, sir," he frowned, "but aren't you going to punish him ... at the very least."

The red-haired captain glowered at the hull technician.

"How about if I decide to send you packing. I'm certain that you had more to do with the incident than I think. I am well aware of your history with hazing and initiation. I had already posted that absolutely no 'thank you sir, may I have another,' welcoming wagons will be tolerated on this vessel under my command ... do I make myself crystal?"

"Yes, sir." Hairybear grumbled. He was a much larger man than Kastos, but the intensity of the captain's stare made him feel much smaller.

"You are dismissed." Kastos wheeled about and walked over to the table to see what Reech had drawn on the sea maps, no longer interested in the idiotic doings of the hull tech. He waited until he is gone and then turned to Trantos, who was sheathing his saber.

"I could not help but notice that he had a sullen, suspicious look in his eye," Trantos warned the captain. "I hope he isn't planning on pulling a plan against you, we should watch him."

"Hmmpfh," Kastos exhaled, "probably nothing more than ransacking through the rest of Turkeyneck's belongings to see what he can keep for himself, but duly noted all the same."

Then the captain returned to the course that his valuable navigator had plotted on the chart sheets, the one that would lead him to the shores of Xoth, the kingdom of the old gods.

3

The night sky became a veil of deepest purple by the time Hairybear went below to the berthing compartments. He planned to catch a little sleep before the twin suns rose. Unmooring a ship was a hard morning's work and he was already tired out from the day's foiled events. He had had high hopes of erasing the navigator's sense of direction with the hazing, because Hairybear did not want to go where Kastos intended. It was a foolhardy quest and would endanger all of the men including him. Since he had nowhere else to go, he was invested in keeping the *Kella* in one piece.

The old man who had been drinking on watch with him crawled out from a hatchway and approached him, asking, "What are you gonna do now?"

Hairybear looked at the little wino with burning contempt.

"I'm gonna get some rest and sleep on it," he growled as he opened the door that led into the seaman division. "Now get the fuck out of my face before I take you topside and throw you overboard to the sharks right along with Turkeyneck."

The old drunk scampered away.

Hairybear found his bunk, crawled into it, clothes and all, then closed his tiny privacy curtain shut.

Dawn brought on a foggy shore filled with a mist that crawled up onto the pier, over the decks and into the vents. This made the interior of the ship clammy and cold. Visibility would be hindered, yet Kastos refused to remain landlocked. Mooring lines were thrown off by the sleepy-eyed crew, then the battered tugboats pushed the larger vessel off from the barnacle-encrusted pier. Then slowly and very tentatively the

Kella navigated its way through the channel. Slowly they moved away from Arpoch's wharf.

In the sky the tandem suns still hid behind a veil of cloud, with only a pale representation of their twin glory exhibited as a ball of orange light and a dim blue glow that ascended into the morning sky.

After a half hour the *Kella* reached the open sea, which was a roiling, blue beast filled with great swells due to the minor seismic activity that always shook the northwestern floor. It was one of the reasons Arpoch and many of the other northlands had been abandoned. Some labeled Kastos a madman, because he had attempted to set sail on these treacherous waters, and his crew even crazier for following him. The men who had never sailed before marveled over the effect, although a few of them became too seasick to do anything other than lie on the poop deck with their heads hanging over the side, puking, while everyone else stepped over them.

Seaman Cosmo shuffled up next to Gank, who was watching the frothy wake of the ship trail off behind them. They stood on top of the bridge, on the signal deck where Gank enjoyed his naps in his little weather shack. Their eyes squinted as the dual suns began to shine a stronger flare upon the early day. Jagged mountains and stone crests peeked out of the fog that covered the departing shore. The land surrounding Arpoch was a yellowed, barren waste wthout a single tree left standing. It was a shame, because once upon a time the hills had been a lush, sequoia-filled habitat, but that was long ago, before the old wars.

"Do you think that the captain has any idea where we are going?" Cosmo asked.

"I don't think that he would be setting out on a journey that has no destination," Gank replied.

Cosmo gave the small man a disapproving glance and then turned to leave. The work of storing the mooring lines back into the hold remained to be finished.

"I heard that he sails for the shores of Xoth ... the continent of the old gods that sits on the edge of the world." Cosmo said to the other toiling seamen down in the hold.

They cried in surprise and protest.

"Yeah ... and between me, you and the bulkheads, Hairybear and I ain't too keen on the idea," Cosmo added.

Gank overheard and surmised that Hairybear was doing more than just organizing hazing operations. He could be stirring up a possible mutiny. The pygmy had friends amongst the crewmembers, but he was ultimately loyal to Kastos. If something was up, Gank would have to keep an eye on things. Chances were definitely good that Hairybear would cause another situation.

Gank watched the waves, his own mind was filled with reservations over where they were heading. Nothing good as far as news went ever came out of the wastelands of the southern pole. It was a place they were well-advised to stay away from. Yet the morning mood among the men was high as the *Kella* sped over the glistening sea. Best he not dwell on matters that he couldn't change even if he wanted.

Kastos, Trantos and Reech were up on the bridgewing of the *Kella* where they watched the horizon as it dipped and rose. Kastos instructed the helmsman, a seasoned mariner who went by the handle of Sharkbait, not to swing the ship about haphazardly. Sharkbait had a bad habit that allowed the ship to roll way too much when he steered it. Everyone could tell when it was his turn at the wheel because everything that wasn't tied down went careening to the deck. Trays, cups and utensils crashed all over the galley. Those who performed tasks stumbled into each other in the passageways cursing and swearing that one of these days Sharkbait was going to live up to his name and be eighty-sixed off the ship's aft end.

"No problem, Cap'n, I got this!"

Kastos rolled his eyes, shook his head and then grasped the multi-colored painted rail as the *Kella* took another lurching tumble over a starboard side swell.

"Gods and demons, man! What did I just say?"

"Sorry, Cap'n" Sharkbait said. Due to lack of teeth he always dropped his "t's"; long ago he had fallen prey to the afflictions known to those who had never seen the ancient artifact known as a toothbrush.

The washed-out port of Arpoch certainly had not yielded a very good batch of seaman for the journey. Kastos felt discouraged over the lack of skills that this crew of degenerates possessed. Nevertheless, they would have to be enough. All the good things of the world, including hardy seamen, were a thing of the past.

Swirling overhead in the ship's windbreak were a number of mutated seagulls cavorting and gliding, and below the draft line, freakish flying fish attached themselves to the wind created near the hull. Behind them the land diminished until no more of it was in sight. They had reached the open sea.

The first day out proved to be uneventful, although after a few hours the ship entered a thick bank of mist near Cisco Point. Kastos commanded Reech to move the craft closer to shore and follow the coast. Here a great rift had been caused, and molten earth had crawled up through crevices to create dangerous, steaming vapors. Also a shelf of razor-sharp teeth made out of rocky crust lay in wait just below the waterline. Strong currents would cause ships to drag their bottoms across those jagged boulders and rip open as if they were made of tin.

By noon the fog burned off and they came within sight of the lonely stretch of shoreline belonging to the dead lands. Here weapons of mass destruction were once tested during the old wars, and forever afterwards caused the place to glow at night. It was infected, a blight on the planet, an incredibly vast contamination zone, yet even though the hills were poisoned with radioactivity, they were still filled with eyes. Cannibal tribes known as Smegs lurked in the maggot holes that filled those rocky crags. Hordes of them survived on captured outsiders or sometimes even each other, they weren't at all partial. They were vicious, savage mutants that fed off human flesh. They had done so for ages, since there wasn't any wildlife left to speak of, and all of the game had been diseased or rendered extinct.

Some of the flesh hunters had also been known to take to the water in gasoline-driven jet rafts that would easily overtake the slower, steam-driven *Kella*. That was extremely rare and highly unlikely, and besides, the *Kella* had a catapult that was very accurate in surface-to-surface warfare.

The water ran off from the dead lands and dumped into the sea, which had ruined the entire section of the coast. All the marine life in these waters suffered from the tainted streams and rivers that flowed through the wastelands into this surf, not only damaged by the aftermath of the bombs, but from a leftover string of half-destroyed chemical plants that still leaked seepage into the earth. Built long before the coalition could stop the enemy constructions, the foothold that was an attempt to secure Greater America's western shore. It had been inevitably uprooted, but at great cost to the land itself. The coalition did what it had to do and used their nukes.

There would be no trolling for supper tonight in these waters.

"They certainly turned these waters into a dump," Trantos said, as they watched the day turn to twilight over this empty, soured ocean.

"That they did," Kastos agreed.

Nightfall brought strange lights into the sky that made the men feel uneasy. Most of them were a superstitious lot, and feared that the gods were warning them to turn back. Kastos did little to allay these fears by putting on a good drunk. After he finished off another bottle of stone liquor he busted out from his cabin and laughed at the men for their deep-seated taboos.

"The Gods are forbidding us to travel through these waters," Cosmo remarked as he pointed towards the overhead spectacle. Great flowering fans of color made designs and shapes in the sky that would have been nothing less than fascinating, if they weren't so foreboding.

Kastos guffawed in the face of fear and lived up to his reputation as a baron of bravado. He thrust the sign of the mortal coil with both hands held up to the sky.

"Fuck 'em!" he shouted.

The men could not help but be rallied by the audacity of Kastos' attitude, and soon they too were passing around strong drink. A song rose as they cheered up from their dirges and restraints, shifting the entire mood of the crew into party mode. The ship was set on autopilot by Reech, so that it stayed on course, and he also stood watch over it while the captain was busy skylarking.

Everyone else was busy making merry, save for Hairybear who glared at all of them from the shadows like a jealous soul. Trantos' keen eyes spotted Hairybear, and so he made a mental note that trouble might come from the hull technician at some point further down the line.

"The men are drunk with the promise of good fortune, but we will keep our own heads level at least, eh?" Gank told Trantos as they watched Kastos throw himself onto his men, who lifted him up and body-carried him across their fingertips as if he were a rock star.

A hatch opened from amidships and a tired, miserable face peered out. It was Eddie Wrichtyrowski, known as "Skee" for short, who worked all day in the galley serving up meals for the crew. Since he had to prepare everything himself, that made him the only one on board who had to wake up before the tandem suns rose at dawn.

"Hey," Skee barked, "You guys mind keeping it down a little, I'm trying to get some rest!"

All of the men nodded apologetically. Even Kastos regained his dignity for a moment and stood fixing himself with the self-admonishment that befit a figure of authority caught in the act of being foolish.

"Yeah, okay," Kastos offered. "No problem, Eddie."

The curmudgeon grunted with satisfaction and then closed the hatchway.

As soon as he was gone the men made noise again, as if they had not even heard Skee's request. Eventually he would return to open the hatch and bark at the men again and again as the party continued all throughout their first night at sea.

The next morning had an abundance of even more clammy fog, and a lot of hung-over crewmembers. The joyous attitude that had spread throughout the ship the prior evening was long gone. Their indulgences had brought on a rough commencement to the day.

"We are still in these filthy waters?" Kastos asked Reech,

who had been checking the latitude with a chronometer. He was making an attempt to survey the twin suns' angle as they broke the horizon. However, the thick fog was hindering the cotton-haired joe from gaining a true fix on the distance between the spheres and the waterline.

Nevertheless, the navigator's uncanny sense of direction held strong.

"Yes," Reech said, "and I believe that we are nearing the haunted shoreline of Saint's Dagger. We will need to be on our guard."

"Kastos, we are picking up readings of toxins in the air now." Gank announced.

"Don the NBC masks ... now!"

No sooner said than done, and the entire crew was putting on their nuclear-biological-chemical warfare gear as they entered the perimeter of the deadly coast. Gank ran up onto the signal shack in order to look through the big scopes at the eerie, ill-defined cliffs of this place, where the receding fog exposed some of Saint's Dagger. Here were rusted, dilapidated billboards displaying bio-hazard symbols that stood as a warning for any would-be trespassers to think twice. Beyond it towered the ruined skyline of a city that appeared to be melted, no doubt by some terrible weapon that was spawned by the sciences of the old war. Rumor control had it that a great shadow resided within that haunted place that bound the spirits of those it killed, keeping them in the hell that it had created. Kastos felt its presence, which alerted him to the fact that whatever it was that lurked in that hole *was also aware of them.*

"We keep right on moving by, gentlemen," Kastos uttered through his muffling gas mask, "this place has worse things than death for those who step on those shores."

Off the starboard side they could see the city up close. A dirty, brown cloud hung over the city as if trying to cloak its terrible secrets. The broken, sheared-off buildings resembled knives that stuck up from its murk; thus Saint's Dagger lived up to its name.

The ship steamed past a long, rocky pier that stretched across the befouled harbor, ending off only a few yards from the *Kella*'s wake. Here was a queer, surrealistic, wrought-iron sculpture of a cone-shaped face mounted on the end of the dock. Pipes and struts were fastened upon this incredibly enormous welded pile, causing macabre whistles as the sea air wafted through them. Its eyes were two great spirals of flattened copper that gave off strange audible vibrations, possibly meant to repel visitors. It was a totem constructed to ward off any would-be explorers looking to uncover the reasons behind the horrific besmirching of this shoreline.

The men felt very unsettled, and one of the crewmembers even ended up stuck with a faulty mask, one that had sprung a leak and caused him to ingest polluted air. Because of that he had to administer a self-injecting serum into his thigh, an antidote against the effects that the chemical-laden atmosphere brought. The sailor was nearly stricken with paralysis before the medicine finally performed its miracle. Fortunately, Kastos had had the insight to provide the medications that were needed for this hazardous voyage.

Other men reported being *tugged at* by invisible, long fingers that belonged to an unseen, menacing force that drilled into their heads and actually yanked on their minds.

"It's trying to pull our souls out of our bodies, but it can't, not if we are still alive," Kastos informed the men. Many of them had horrified looks upon their faces, aghast that their captain had brought them so close to such a hellish place.

Trantos reached into his black cloak and pulled forth a flute and held it to his lips. He played a haunting, gypsy-style melody that seemed to ward off the terrible sensation the men were feeling. It also masked the weird sounds emanating from the iron sentinel. Kastos commanded that more speed be put to the ship at once so that they could be released from the grip of whatever force lurked beneath that eerie city.

The *Kella* had finally passed beyond the proximity of Saint's Dagger and its malevolent denizens. Now they were able to unfasten the straps to their NBC masks and peel them off from their sweaty heads. The air was still enhanced with chemical-laced purple haze, although now at a safer level. They could taste it in their mouths and feel weird sensations going up and down their spines. Kastos even imagined oval, bean-shaped creatures doing indescribably blasphemous acts in his mind's eye. They were the harbingers of madness, ones that could not be cured by a simple antidote.

Once clear from the shadow place the invaders fled from Kastos' psyche, and the sea wind picked up and began to blow away the dead fog, pushing it behind the colorful frigate as the *Kella* sailed onward.

4

The fresh new wind soon became violent, and once they had passed out of the undersea fangs of rock, the ship sluiced out into a gale that had started to brew. Storm clouds formed that were filled with flashes of lightning. Yet, that wasn't the real peril. On the sea's western horizon, a dark veil of cumulus advanced, which was the heart of the true storm.

"HAIL! HAIL IS COMING, TAKE COVER!"

A scraggly sailor called "Storch" cried from his lookout point that was a makeshift crow's nest fashioned out of a defunct radar balcony. After issuing the warning he retracted his scope and quickly began to descend the ropes, similar to a spider crawling. It was clear to everyone by now that the approaching wall of darkness was in fact a sheet of precipitation.

The men took cover as large balls of layered ice fell out of the black sky, pelting them as they attempted to secure a few loose items at the last second. Kastos bellowed for everyone to make for the ship's interior before the ocean itself responded to this blustery climate shift. Thirty-foot-high swells made the *Kella* rock to and fro like a cork upon the waves.

"This is madness!" Reech yelled as he pinwheeled his arms, lost his balance and fell over. Fortunately, he fell only onto a pile of folded canvas tarps and several life preservers that were in his path. He had merely hurt his navigational dignity more than anything else.

"Hey," Trantos said, grinning at the fallen cotton-haired-joe. "You all right there, old fella?"

"Yeah, yeah, yeah," Reech retorted with a sullen tone. Then he stood back on his feet and silently swore to make certain that he had a strong handhold the next time the boat took a roll.

Abruptly a loud, crunching, snapping sound came from beneath the aft end of the *Kella*, and Kastos knew that it denoted a broken rudder, which was terrible news. It meant that the ship was at the complete mercy of nature's wrath.

"We will lose course," Kastos announced. "We have no wheel."

There was nothing they could do. The men would have to ride out the gale. They were in store for a long, tiresome night of tossing and dipping. Seasickness would take its toll on most of the lot, who had never been on the water in their lives until this voyage.

"We must turn back," Cosmo bawled, *"the old gods will not allow us into their midst. We shall not be granted access to the forbidden shores."*

Everyone gathered inside of the *Kella*'s darkened interior and looked to Kastos, as if expecting and hoping he would agree to beg forgiveness from the gods for giving them the mortal coil and save them from this storm.

"We have no choice," Kastos stated. "The rudder has snapped ... we are now at the mercy of the fates."

The men murmured in fear and disappointment. Only Hairybear remained silent as he glared at the captain from the shadows, with burning, vengeful eyes.

After a hellish night of rocking, rolling and battering, along with the stench of vomit from all of the landlubbers puking, the storm finally began to abate. And the sky cleared and showed off a blazing pair of suns.

The boat drifted into waters that were smooth as glass, where repairs could easily be made to the busted rudder by Hairybear and his trusty hull-technician team. Meanwhile, the rest of the crew had engaged themselves in fishing off the sides of the boat, a good idea since most of the food in the hold had been ruined by seawater, soaked from a leak made by the beating taken from the typhoon.

After a few hours the ship was back underway, using the steam-powered engines since the wind was nil. Soon they came upon a completely destroyed fleet of ships that had apparently been dashed to ruin on some sharp rocks, most likely from the storm. Kastos delegated Gank to take a team of men and look for things that might be worth salvaging. They returned hours later with a long boat filled with more food, clothing, tools, and some medical supplies. There were no signs of any survivors or of any bodies. All of the dead had probably been scavenged by carrion crabs which were running everywhere on the rocks and below the water's surface.

The crew found a strange metal machine with red and black claws attached to it by cables, possibly for interrogation purposes, along with many other bizarre devices. However, the most peculiar thing of all was a long metal cylinder, a tank of some sort, posted with a bizarre, diamond-shaped emblem that identified it, although no one could understand the writing.

"What do you think is in that cylinder?" Kastos asked Reech.

"*Sorcery*," the old cotton-haired joe ejaculated. His eldritch ways always gave him a paranoid outlook when it came to things that confounded or baffled him. Although the metal tank *did* seem sinister, still Kastos would not part with it, thinking he might be able to fetch a pretty penny for it at the next barter port. So on board it went.

It was Hairybear who had found the strange, tube-shaped canister. He was always looking to tinker with the old equipment and devices of the past. With that cylinder for instance, he had found something that only he alone would recognize as a valuable item, good for a rainy day perhaps.

"We are missing two seamen," Gank reported. Kastos looked up at him dully. He and Reech were poring over charts and maps, making new coordinates. They glanced up with dour faces.

"More than likely they fell overboard," Kastos said with a solemn voice.

Sure enough, after Gank had taken head count two more times, there was no sign of Storch, who was in the crow's nest. Or of Eddie Wrichtyrowski, who was the cook. Gank was really sad about that, because he loved Skee's vittles, and had the big, round, chocolate-colored pygmy belly to prove it.

Nothing to be done about it. There was no way they would

ever find the missing men after the storm. Kastos held an assembly later that day and spoke a few words in their honor and then wished them passage with ease into the realm of the spirits.

Kastos caught sight of Hairybear whispering something into Cosmos' ear. He could not help feeling suspicious when he looked at those two men communicating so secretively.

"Captain, look!" Trantos shouted. "It's a boat!"

Everyone who had been paying heed to Kastos' speech now turned their heads to the port side. Indeed, there was a small craft bobbing up and down on the twinkling water. The setting suns had cast such an intense corona of light on the horizon that the craft was difficult to pinpoint inside the glare until it came closer. It appeared heavily laden, overloaded and ready to be swamped by the lapping waves that spilled over its sides. Yet, not one of the refugees waved nor cheered nor showed any kind of enthusiasm at all towards being rescued. Perhaps they were too dazed by whatever ordeal the wrath of the storm had brought on them to even care.

"Jeez," Gank remarked, "*look* at them."

The crew of the *Kella* nearly had to catch their breath when the newcomers came closer. Their faces had a strange, fish-like look to them, some more so than others. A few of them who did not wear garments high enough to cover their necks, appeared to have gills. Kastos thought that they were quite unique, but if he was any kind of a judge of character upon first impressions, he would have to say that all of these survivors had a perturbed scowl upon their mugs. Almost as if they resented the *Kella* being in their path.

"I don't like them," Cosmo said quietly to Hairybear, so that only he could hear. "I don't think that the captain should let them on board." With a furtive pout on his face, he looked this way and that as if to make certain that nobody was watching, but again, Kastos caught their exchange. However, he did not voice any admonishment, because in all actuality he had to agree. The fish-men indeed seemed quite unsavory as well as possibly troublesome.

Then the captain of the *Kella* espied the beautiful woman

who sat in their midst. Kastos was suddenly enamored with the beauty of her luxurious dark hair and sun-bronzed skin. She charmed and enticed him with one look, yet it wasn't only her shapely body and angelic face that held him in thrall, it was a pair of bracelets wrought of gold that she wore on her wrists. On each one were hieroglyphics that Kastos recognized. They were engravings and symbols written in the language of Xoth. It was the secret language that came from the forbidden shore of the old gods.

"Let them come aboard," Kastos ordered, "but bring the woman to my quarters. I wish to speak with her."

Within a minute, the *Kella* came up alongside the small craft and began to bring the refugees on board. The men who helped them did little to conceal their disgruntlement. All the while they muttered protests under their breath. The newcomers had a strong odor, the smell of sea mud at low tide. And their faces were indeed akin to those of marine creatures. Except the girl, who was so fair that the captain of the *Kella* was unable to keep from wondering how she became shipwrecked with these weirdlings.

5

The tandem suns sank below the horizon of the multicolored waters, and a partial moon that resembled the edifice of a rotted corpse began to rise. The crew began to relax as the ship slowly cruised through pleasant, calm waters for a change. They grilled the fish that they had caught, and the musicians played some music. Trantos and Reech milled about with the rest of the crew, who attempted to befriend the fish-men, who called themselves the fathomers or the deep ones. Gank, with his cheery, jovial nature, also had a hand in helping everyone make friends. Even Cosmo left Hairybear alone to wallow in his own funk, while he had a drink with the men.

The raven-haired female who had been escorted by Gank to the captain's quarters stood waiting alone outside the door. She did not knock.

Kastos was ready. He had already heard the chaperoning seaman's heavy footfalls walk away. So he grasped the door handle in his hand, and nearly hesitated, because he felt a wave of heavy, ominous, energy that came from beyond the wooden barrier. He thought that there must be a force-field around her, because he was almost thrown back by her presence.

Kastos opened the door.

Seeing her up close was a hundred times more toxic than spotting her from the boat. Her eyes were liquid, dark, beguiling and warm—*knowing*, he thought, those eyes were all-knowing.

Her body was slender, yet full. It moved in ways Kastos had not seen in over a year. She was a woman! He struggled with an attempt to keep his growing appetite suffused with divine purpose so he wouldn't fall into her charms, which of course, he already had.

Kastos watched her as she sat as intently as a hawk. Then he waited a moment until she seemed relaxed, and began to question her.

"I want to know about the bracelets you are wearing." He started to pour them both a drink. "Will you tell me where they came from?"

She took the drink and rather than sip from it she allowed it only to swirl around in her glass. Kastos was astonished to see it go down, as if she wafted up its vapors while it evaporated, indulging on the cocktail with some strange mutant-witchery.

"Why?" she replied with a voice that purred, answering his question with a question.

He pointed to the inscriptions on the bracelets. They gleamed enchantingly in the candlelight of this inner cabin. Intertwining tendrils of serpent, vine and script had been scribed upon the accessories' surface with such fine detail that Kastos thought there was no way that they could have been rendered by humans.

"Don't you understand the legends written upon these?" Kastos asked, "It is the writing of the old gods, this speech comes from the forbidden realm of Xoth."

She placed her now-empty wine goblet onto the oaken table, and gave no reply, only batted her eyes. Kastos quickly glanced at her heaving bosom and felt that he *wanted* her in a way he had nearly forgotten, after having spent so many long months at sea. So he softened his approach.

"Tell me your name."

"Keisha."

His eyes roved freely now over her suntanned shoulders, examining her elegant neck and shapely form that was barely concealed inside of a sarong fashioned out of torn blue rags. Clothing was made from whatever you could lay your hands on in these after-times.

The woman stood up from her chair and walked over to him, allowing her makeshift dress to drop and reveal her gorgeous body. Kastos took her right there, without further invitation, his unbridled lust was now in control. Stripping off his fatigues, he stood ready with his manhood at attention. He then removed everything from the table with a single swipe of his hand. Maps, charts, instruments and bottle of stone liquor scattered and crashed to the deck. Then with a savage, passionate embrace he threw her onto the board and with a slow, delicious thrust he entered her. He made love to her with more intensity than he had ever known, because in his heart he recognized her as someone whose veins flowed with divine blood. Keisha was a conduit that brought out more stamina in him than he thought was possible. She was different than any other woman, something deep within her was hidden, and he intended to find out what it was.

Finally, after what seemed like hours, they lay exhausted, now in the bunk that his cabin provided. They talked about his past. He noted that she did not care to talk about herself nor where she had really come from. She only told him that it was from a very faraway place, and that he would not understand.

Kastos did not push the issue, not yet at least.

Afterwards they walked out on deck among the men who were steaming fish and tending to their barbecues. It was a nice change from the tensions they had endured upon leaving Arpoch. The fish-men proved to be excellent anglers as well as cooks. Their art with the flavorings made many friends among the crew. Everyone was gaining a swift fellowship with one another as the common interest of food paved the way. Even the weather was in tune with the idyllic atmosphere. A sweet, caressing tropical breeze began to stir as the ship sailed through waters near the equatorial dividing line. On the galley tables sat an array of different bounty, enough to satisfy any hunger cravings. These waters were filled withnettles eels and purple crab, along with a vast abundance of salt-water trout. All evening the air was filled with the tantalizing aroma of sea food grilling and broiling away as the *Kella* went further south.

The next day was uneventful unless you counted all the action going on inside the captain's quarters between Kastos and his new lady friend. The two of them hardly ever left the cabin. They would roll in the hay, then they ate some fried snettle eel, then rolled in the hay again, then looked at some maps, then rolled in the hay an additional time, then afterwards drank some stone liquor, and then, of course, they rolled in the hay once more.

The following day clear skies and fair winds brought them into turquoise-blue waters where schools of ivory dolphins danced on the waves in front of the *Kella*'s prow. They raced effortlessly ahead of the boat as it sped over the cresting, salty froth, leaping and frolicking in glistening, water-splashed arcs.

The *Kella*'s newly repaired rudder was working even better than before, and the ship cruised at an easy thirty-plus knots. Still, the animals swam so quickly that it seemed as if the frigate were standing still. More rainbow flying fish were also caught up in the draft, dazzling with their sparkling, crystal butterfly wings. They soared with ease alongside the boat in the ocean's spray.

That night it was Gank's turn at the wheel. Unfortunately, he was not used to such a boring watch. That, plus the feasts of booze and fish had taken its toll. He had dozed off to sleep.

Kastos noticed that the constellations overhead were upside down. The ship had turned about and was now off course.

"GANK! Wake up man … what the hell!"

"HUH! What! Oh! Shit! Sorry, Captain!"

Hairybear, who happened to be standing nearby, chuckled.

"Good thing it isn't time of war … you'd be shot!"

Gank gave the sarcastic hull tech a feral look.

Keisha stepped up to the captain, pressed herself against his mighty chest and held up her arms to display the golden bracelets. She showed him the sides with the finely written arabesque runes.

"Do you really know the way to the lost shore of Xoth?" Keisha asked, almost mockingly.

Something in her smile told Kastos that she knew more about their destination than his own navigator did. He eyed her suspiciously.

"Yes, mistress, what do *you* know?"

She then gave him a feline look that would make a black cat envious.

"I know nothing," she said, and whirled away from him, her eyes veiled and doused of any inclination towards prior interest in this present conversation.

Kastos followed after her. He had no intention of letting that be the final word in the matter of this voyage.

Gank let out a deep breath, relieved now to be out of the limelight. He resumed his duty with a newfound vigor, and this time did not fall asleep.

Kastos caught up to Keisha at the railing of the poop deck. He turned her around by the shoulders and lifted her arm to look at the bracelets.

There was the fine outline of a map, one that depicted a route to the lost shore of Xoth.

Kastos felt his breath quicken. This woman had a free pass to the source of his dreams.

"You may find the forbidden shore, yet you still need help passing the sentries at the door, particularly with Syryops who is the lord of Xoth. Syryops is a terrible titan who can destroy you with one glance. Syryops is the keeper of the gate." Keisha said forbiddingly.

Kastos needed time to ponder these words. He was certain that they were crucial to the outcome of his quest. One more thing that Kastos the high adventurer was certain of, was that he wanted the golden bracelets even more than he wanted her.

DON
PARESI

6

Ahead of the ship was the great port city of Avanex, a huge trading province built by the desert people who had come to settle here on the ocean. Its great harbor was protected from the nomadic cannibal smegs by a hot radiation zone that girdled its land borders. The only way to enter was through the harbor and that was well-guarded by the inhabitants who had bowstring catapults mounted upon the walls, as well as three armored ships. One of the rebuilt vessels even had a Gatlin gun that shot fifty caliber slugs made out of pig iron.

The Greater American Jack staff and colors on the *Kella* were well recognized as "friendlies" to the dusky-skinned Avanex race. The annual festival of New Sky was underway, a time of celebration. It was a good time to make a port visit.

"Wow, looks like the party is on, eh?" Gank said.

The ramparts and pyramids of the city were full of people drinking and dancing. Multicolored torches dotted the skyline, lighting up the city as twilight arrived.

The beaches were filled with celebration and flowing taps of fresh stone liquor that the crew could not wait to drink. There were pigs roasting and beautiful girls in nothing but thongs dancing with acrobatic fire-eaters. The sailors were anxious to go and spend their trading chits.

One of the three ships that guarded the harbor drifted up to the *Kella* to address the captain. Kastos stood on the quarterdeck as the immaculately feathered chieftains came aboard. The main man, a tall, thin, copper-colored Indian named Chobaldo, was apparently the spokesman. He could understand the common speech and could understand Kastos' language. He held up his hand and used the friendly signal of a world party greeting, but ironically began to speak using grave tones.

"These are tense times my friends, the sea is filled with enemies, we had to be sure that you are not Sarthogs." He waved his arm out at the three armed Avanex ships that flanked the *Kella*.

"Sarthogs?" Trantos, who was standing nearby, inquired.

"Yes," Kastos answered, "I know of them, they are the half-frog/half-man people of Tsin who are a very, unfriendly bunch of assholes."

The brightly feathered ambassador looked at the half-men-half-fish people on the ships poop deck with suspicious eyes.

"I see that you have met up with some of the fathomers."

"Yes," Kastos replied, "a weird looking entourage, yet for the most part they don't seem to care about anything other than angling for their supper, eating and sleeping. I don't think that they want to come ashore. I believe they would rather remain on ship and throw lines into the harbor. The sea bounty here is exotic as well as plentiful."

"Indeed." Chobaldo said, well aware of the massive shoals of salt trout that migrated through these waters. There were also a company of lobster-turtles, and even one or two gigantic yellow sharks just within sight. Large, gas-filled blowfish lamps that were tethered to the boat hovered over the water's surface, illuminating the incredible exhibition of nature's aquarium below.

"Very well," Chobaldo said, "I don't see the harm in that. It's probably best that they don't come ashore. Some of the guests at the celebration might not take too kindly to them. We don't want any problems."

Kastos nodded in agreement.

"However," Chobaldo added, "the rest of you are welcome."

The city of Avanex was nothing less than marvelous. It had been created out of the skeletal remains of a once great metropolis, one that had fallen during the old wars. The skilled builders of *these* latter days had wrought a spectacular design out of the ruins. It appeared gorgeous from the ship, lit up from thousands of torches from the many levels where people danced and celebrated. Loud music pumped out of speakers fashioned together out of whatever had been leftover from the destruction. Platforms had been installed upon tall, artful pyramid structures, so that the citizens of Avanex could practice heliotherapy, an ancient form of sun healing. Unfortunately the practice was nearly abolished, due to the fact that the corona of the twin suns had grown to dangerous proportions.

After the ship dropped anchor, Kastos, Keisha and the

crewmen of the *Kella* went ashore to enjoy the festival, where any number of open banquets were available for seating. Kastos particularly liked the dancing girls.

"Maybe I should dance for you later, eh Kastos?" Keisha winked.

"You don't have to be a dancer to dance for me baby."

She giggled against his arm. He was falling for her, and that might not be such a bad thing, Kastos thought to himself.

Back on ship, Hairybear, who had decided to not go on shore either, stayed below decks until the main bulk of the crew had left for the feast. Once he had heard the concerts and crowds jeering and cheering he commenced his little prank that he had planned. He intended to use one of the devices obtained during the salvage operation.

On the topmost signal deck was a little staging platform that Hairybear had set up. An electronic device was beneath it, attached to a wire that came all the way over to where he sat with a remote control in his hand. His fat thumb was at the ready to press the red SEND button. Mounted upon the platform disc was an incendiary-driven, cardboard rocket. A mischievous smile spread across his face.

Back on land, Kastos and crew were still having a grand time, when suddenly their table was surrounded by a group of the copper-hued, exquisitely groomed Indians. All of them were armed with sharp javelins.

Chobaldo appeared among them, with his hands raised, as if he had an important announcement.

"You have to leave the island."

"Why?" Kastos asked.

"Someone has fired an object from your ship!"

Kastos looked out at the bay. He could see a stream of fire shoot up into the darkness that left a definitive burning trail.

"Holy shit!" Reech uttered.

Something had been fired from the boat, and Kastos and his party must be removed for fear that the people would react. Looting and rioting had already begun. As the crowd control was too thin to control an insurgence, this had to be squelched immediately.

"I am sorry," Chobaldo apologized, "but you must leave the celebration immediately."

"Understood," Kastos offered, "we were on our way out anyway."

On a trash barge, rather than the nice welcome-wagon boat the Indians had offered earlier, the crew of the *Kella* headed back to the ship. Trantos stopped munching on a barbecued mutant-monkey-tail-on-a-stick long enough to ask who might've been stupid enough amongst the crew to commit an international incident of such a nature.

Everyone shook their head, no one had a clue.

Once the men had all been placed back on ship, the trash barge returned to the docks, and the three defense ships closed off the harbor to ensure that the *Kella* was on its way.

"I guess they mean business," Gank said, then hauled his pygmy frame up the ladder to the signal shack, where he raised the appointed flags. Kastos and the men weighed anchor and with heavy hearts, left behind them forever the celebrated city of Avanex.

Kastos and the crew sought the perpetrator behind the rocket launch, as soon as the *Kella* weighed anchor and was underway. Hairybear had been busy nurturing a rumor that the fish-men were behind the whole thing. He meant to make the crew, who already had a base dislike for the bizarre anglers, follow along with his pied-piper's call and also accuse the newcomers.

"It's a lie," Keisha protested, "they have no knowledge of such science."

Kastos also did not believe that the fish-men were responsible. When the launch pad and wires had been found, he was convinced that someone with technical knowledge, someone like an electronics sorcerer would have to be to blame, somebody who was educated in the rules of physics—somebody such as Cosmo or Hairybear. Those two were skilled when it came to that.

Kastos also remembered the way they appeared to be whispering and plotting something the day of the memorial service. Then he brushed the thought away. Perhaps he was just being paranoid.

Yet, there was nothing to be done. Time would have to tell, Kastos thought.

"HOLY SHIT! WILL YOU LOOK AT ALL THAT FISH!" Gank shouted as he gawked at the hold filled with seafood. The fathomers had been plenty busy angling while the rest of the crew partied in Avanex.

Kastos smiled, but he wanted to do nothing but fall fast asleep in his cabin, where Keisha had been waiting for him to finish his investigations. After they had another session of mad, sweaty sex he fell right to sleep, and then began to dream.

It was more like a nightmare than a dream. Kastos walked through a dark tunnel filled with terrifying faces and shadows towards a dim, green ambient light. Within that subtle glow at the far end of the corridor he could see a figure coming towards him. It was Keisha, yet she appeared different. Her eyes and hair seemed faded and gray and her skin was no longer tanned and golden. Instead she was pale white, with dark veins showing under her skin. Her flesh had a mottled, decayed texture, but her face still exhibited intense feelings for him, perhaps even love.

Keisha had something in her hands that she was holding out to him. It was her golden bracelets. Kastos took them and examined them carefully in the darkness of the eerily lit corridor.

"Choose me," Keisha directed, while looking at him through huge eyes that were more like the dark holes of an old knotted tree trunk. "Please choose me … I love you Kastos, I will love you forever!"

The bracelets began to brighten as they lit up with a yellow, neon glow that revealed equations and formulas to the captain. A span of information was embedded into the metal. Vital knowledge that was much too vast for the simplicity of a mere mortal soul to comprehend. Yet, Kastos still somehow retained the wisdom deep within his inner mind.

Then Keisha reached out to hold him with arms that were filled with decomposition and wriggling, flesh-eating worms. Kastos shrank back, fearing the touch of those rotted limbs.

Abruptly a horn blared from somewhere inside of this deep, dark place, a sound that chilled Kastos to the bone. It was a lonely, forlorn bellow, monstrous and alien. Then long, whip-like tendrils uncoiled and reached out from the cavern beyond the woman, and enwrapped her corpse-like figure.

They began to drag her backwards, yanking her down into the tunnel, to wherever the source was that those long whips came from.

"Choose me! Please choose me when the door is open, Kastos!"

Kastos wanted to drop the bracelets and reach out to save her, but she was drawn back into the blackness by those strands before he could act. Soon her ghostly form vanished from his sight. Then only the diminished echo of her words remained.

"Choose me ..."

Kastos awoke and heard the sound of Keisha's heavy breathing next to him. He caressed her with his palm, feeling her smooth, supple thigh, her voluptuous hip, and wondered to himself how such a horrific dream of her could have been concocted.

Of course I would choose you. I can't imagine how you can think that there might be any choice in the matter.

His passion for her was inflamed.

She moved a little in her sleep, and then in a whispering voice she spoke from the deepest portion of her brain.

"I can open the door, I can help you make it past the guardian of the gates, but only if you choose me."

His blood froze at the mere mention of the words *choose me* coming from her very mouth. These things lay half-remembered in his mind. How could she know all of these things, especially when she herself lay deep in slumber? Did they experience the same dream?

"I choose you Keisha," Kastos proclaimed, although he was uncertain what all of it meant even still. "I choose you."

Suddenly a metallic, clanking sound surprised Kastos, as the bracelets opened and fell from her wrists to the floor. He looked at them dumbly at first, and then climbed out of bed to pick them up. Then he quietly placed them on the nightstand. After that he checked to see if she had awakened, but she hadn't. So he went back under the covers and soon fell asleep himself, only after wondering ever so slightly why the bracelets had come undone the moment he spoke "I choose you." Then he dropped off, and this time there were no dreams.

7

Keisha rose first the next morning. It was hot, stagnant and still. The rising suns were blazing down in all their glory today.

Kastos opened his eyes to see the woman leaning over him, fully dressed and tending to the porthole curtain. He felt disappointed that she was up and about already and did not want to remain in bed with him for some extra-curricular morning activities. The waters were calm and most of the crew was asleep.

"These are for you," Keisha said, "they are yours to keep."

She held the bracelets out to him. He took them wordlessly.

"You shall be able to study the writings on them now," Keisha said. "The knowledge will guide you through many obstacles."

And then without any further word she left the cabin and closed the door behind her, leaving Kastos puzzled and alone.

He rose to the job of commandeering his vessel. The men were already drained from the heat. It would be worse by noon.

"Kastos, the men have sighted a school of pink whales."

There were several massive shapes slowly moving by, too close for comfort. Fortunately for the ship, the enormous beasts were moving away. One of them could swallow the *Kella* whole. Kastos had no desire to engage in a confrontation with such gargantuan sea beasts.

As the ship steamed on through the tropics, Kastos noticed that Keisha was keeping her distance, staying below decks in the galley most of the day. So he did the same and spent time on the bridge, trying to decipher the engravings on the bracelets she had bestowed upon him. Reech offered little help, but soon the ship was navigating on a correct southeasterly course.

"We will be heading into the island chain of Valegueana," Reech said. "It is sketchy territory."

Trantos, who was chewing on a piece of squid jerky, walked over, his hand resting on the hilt of his bejeweled sword.

"I'd feel safer chasing after the pink whales." he confessed.

"LAND HO," they all heard the new lookout yell from up on his perch. The sound of his cry brought everyone out on deck to see the first of the islands in the great string.

"Look at the waterfalls! Ice-cold fresh water, men," Gank exclaimed, as he beheld the fantastic islet with its great swards of jungle, mountains and cascading rivers. The pygmy was extremely excited to go ashore. He had changed into his recreational attire already. "There must be game too, maybe we will find some game. I could go for some roast pig." Slung around his small, round, ebony form were a longbow and a quiver of arrows. In his hands he held a long javelin. Cosmo and the others chuckled about how he would most likely be run right over by a charging warthog if he came across one.

"Fuck you guys," Gank muttered.

The ship had been securely anchored and the men began to lower their own two longboats. As usual, the Fathomers set about angling off the ship, showing no interest in going ashore along with the rest of the men.

"Funky fish-men," Trantos uttered.

Keisha finally approached Kastos, marking a change after the strange cold shoulder she had given him earlier.

"Do not go ashore, Kastos," she warned, "It will not be safe."

Anger flickered in the tall, long-haired, big-piped captain's eyes for a millisecond. Then he composed himself before allowing his temper to flare. Still, his words held an icy tinge to them.

"No, Keisha, I think that it will be okay, best I go keep an eye on the crew if there is danger afoot. The men have sailed a long way with no refreshment. We all need this. You should come too."

She shook her head, and implored him once more to reconsider, to let them go under Trantos' guard. Kastos half expected her to use her charms to make him comply, but she did not. Instead she exhibited that same expressionless stare, that same frosty attitude, and because that was the wrong way to bring him to rein, he ignored her. So even more discouraged than before, Kastos figured that a cold waterfall shower was exactly what he needed.

Later, after cooling off, he would offer her a compromise that might open a door between them, something to bridge the gap that remained between them ever since the dream last night, when she had said, *Choose me.*

"Go then, but keep a watch out for yourself ... the island feels wrong somehow ... I can sense a binding, something here is enchanted."

She grasped the bracelets on his arms. He almost thought that she was going to embrace him.

"Let me hold one of the bracelets. We will be able to use them to communicate if there's trouble."

Without hesitation, he offered her one. She put it on her left wrist, the opposite of the one he had on his right.

Kastos nodded to her, then went over the side and ordered the winchman to lower his boat.

As they oared towards the sun-soaked beach that ringed the lagoon, Kastos felt content enough with their little talk. Also, he was partly relieved that he could go and attend to his crewmembers, and not allow their loyalty to falter. Kastos needed a tight ship and a tight crew to complete this lengthened voyage.

"I must warn everyone to be on their guard," Kastos ordered once they reached the sand, "I will take Edison and Miguel; Reech, you go with Trantos and the others; Hairybear and Gank will stay by the boats. Once we have bathed in the springs we will send relief for you so that you may refresh yourselves."

"I want to hunt boar," Gank announced. "We're starving."

Kastos smiled at the little, meatball-shaped man who hardly looked starved. He was always stuffing his little bearded face with fried snettle eel.

"We are almost there!" Kastos said.

The men cheered in unison, saluting the sky with the mortal coil.

Kastos had reservations about leaving Hairybear to watch the boats. However, he still did not have any concrete proof that the hull technician was responsible for the infamous rocket launch in Avanex. So he let the matter go and instead of worrying about it he lay on a nice flat rock watching the multicolored clouds pass by. They cruised under the dual suns and made interesting shapes to muse upon. Edison, Miguel and the others were busy having wrestling competitions and performing other feats of strength.

On the western side of the island, where Trantos and Reech explored, was another set of pools with waterfalls to enjoy.

"Wooooo Hoooooo!" Trantos whooped as he peeled off his Zorro suit and jumped buck naked into the azure water. Reech picked his way in slowly, like a girl, still wearing his one pair of gray briefs. The old cotton-haired joe was a little bit more conservative.

Back at the boats, Gank and Hairybear sat under the shade of a huge rock. Gank listened to the sound of his stomach growling in disdain, which made Hairybear increasingly annoyed.

"Why don't you go ahead, I think I got this ... I'm not much for skinny dipping," the rugged hull tech said.

Gank looked at him warily.

"Are you sure that it's alright?"

"Yeah, go" he grumbled, "go get a pig!"

Gank leaped to his feet, grabbed up his javelin and went running into the thicket.

Back on the western side of the island Reech, Trantos and the other men rested after cooling off. They had found an interesting spider web and were tossing little hermit crabs into it so that they could watch the resident arachnid do its job of wrapping them up. They were amazed at how fast the bloated, purple, radiation-altered creature packaged and then injected poison into each crab, paralyzing it for later.

"That's crazy," Cosmo said.

"Do you think one of us should go and relieve Gank and Hairybear?" Reech offered.

"Naw, I think Kastos is gonna have Edison and Miguel do it. Let's just kick back for a while more while we can."

"I'm getting hungry," Reech moaned.

"Yeah me too—"

Suddenly Trantos was cut off, startled, because a huge animal had suddenly burst out of the foliage. It was a wild pig. It went running by them and disappeared into the bush again.

"What the fuck!" Trantos exclaimed.

Three seconds later a short, sweating pygmy holding a spear thrust forth from the palm trees. It was Gank, chasing the razorback. Apparently he had already been relieved from boat watch.

"GET THAT PIG!" the small brown man shouted.

"What the double-fuck?" Trantos blurted again, now grabbing his attire and dressing himself in a flash.

"Roast pig is on the menu, boys!" Reech stood up and began to lope in Gank's direction after the pig, and as he moved in haste, the strange gait in his walk became more pronounced. The rest of the men began to follow. Trantos himself was bringing up the rear. Soon all of the men chased after the promise of a rib dinner, with their mouths watering.

They followed the beast with no regard to the fact that they were going deeper into the jungle. Soon the boar had outdistanced the seamen through thick underbrush. They gave up and took time out to catch their breath.

"FUCK!" Gank threw a little tantrum, his dream of bacon and ham having eluded his grasp. He broke his javelin over his knees and tossed the pieces into the ferns.

"This sucks," Reech moaned, "and it's hot as hell."

"I can see something," Trantos said, whose eyes were as sharp as his sword. He pushed his way through a the dangling fronds of long stemmed flowers, and came out into a vast clearing that opened out into a botanical paradise. There were droves of tropical flora gone wild here from the old radiation. A gorgeous garden skirted a large pool that was almost a small lake. Here and there were the ruins of ornately carved limestone buildings that had the appearance of old temple grounds. To Trantos they resembled the structures designed by the ancient guild of freemasons, before the old wars.

Scattered across the globe in remote places such as this there were secret hideaways dedicated to studying the practice of alchemy unhindered, and without persecution. Away from the prying eyes of the exclusionists who were always attempting to harness the secret skills of the sect.

All that remained was mostly rubble, except for the rugged foundations. There was only one immense, gleaming structure that towered over the lake.

"If my eyes don't deceive me, I would have to say that thing over there is made out of fucking gold!"

Nobody paid attention to what Trantos was saying because they were overwhelmed with hunger and more interested in the swaying jungle trees that were laden with bundles of long purple bananas.

Minutes later the crewmen had succeeded in harvesting enough to fill their bellies. The fruit was full, ripe and hard to resist; it was almost as if the bananas were magical.

Trantos was still enamored with the structure made of shining, sun-splashed gold. He stood on the edge of the built pool, staring at it with one hand shielding his eyes. Bright, scintillating star beams of light flashed from it, making it difficult for him to gaze at the pool for too long.

"After we've indulged ourselves of these tropical delights, I say we take a closer look at that thing," Reech said, before biting into the plump, juice-filled fruit. "Maybe it's a temple that the Masonics filled with valuables before the war. Some might still be intact. It doesn't appear as if land forces came through here. All of the buildings that were ruined still have furnishings and equipment was left untouched."

Trantos nodded his head. He liked the idea.

Gank strolled over, no longer dejected from losing his warthog. The exotic bananas fed his appetite for the time being. So he opted out of further quests and lay down on the white sands surrounding the glassy pool.

"After I take a little break … I feel a little sleepy."

"Yeah, me too," Reech said, also plopping himself down onto the sand beneath the shade of a huge palm.

All of the men had the same idea, only Trantos wasn't drowsy as the rest of the men. He appeared unaffected. He was sure that it was because he did not eat any of the purple bananas. He smiled over their laziness, as if they were all a bunch of louts.

Trantos shrugged and then decided to trek around the large body of water to explore the colossal gold mystery, as the crewmembers reclined after their meal and began to fall fast asleep.

8

On the opposite side of the island Kastos and his men had grown bored and began to seek out Trantos and his men. Before long they came to the same pool where the others were eating the bizarre fruit, appearing over fatigued and ready for sleep.

Kastos was annoyed with their laggardness.

"Here now, turn about men," he said, as he kicked a banana out of Gank's hand, waking him up from what appeared to be a drugged sleep, but only momentarily. The pygmy began to fall out once again.

"GANK!" Kastos yelled. The pygmy snapped to a sitting pose, trying to shake off the malaise. "Where's Trantos?"

The small negro pointed over to the monolith of gold that twinkled in the mid-afternoon sun.

"I think he went over to see what that thing is ..."

Kastos felt the single bracelet that was still clasped to his scabbard as it started to tingle, and in his head he could hear Keisha's voice giving him a warning.

Beware Kastos ... there is danger all around you.

On the far side of the pool, Trantos' curiosity soon turned to fascination when he saw upon closer inspection that the structure was the hunched-over form of a giant. It was a massive statue of a big gold man formed out of numerous ingots fused together into a colossal shape.

Trantos was alerted suddenly, when he heard the sound of metal bending and wrenching, as the golden statue lifted its enormous head, and looked right at him.

"No ... by the great rift ... it cannot be ... *alive!"*

Maybe not, but because of the arcane magic arts that the

Masonic alchemists had practiced, the thing could animate. It rose now to a full height of over one hundred feet, and began to walk with great, thunderous strides. Trantos began to run back to warn the men on his side, still not seeing the other group, or Kastos addressing Gank.

"Wake up you fools! Wake up! It's the gold man and he is coming. Wake up!"

Try as he did, it was no use. The men had fallen too deeply into slumber. They woke up slowly, dazedly, some not at all. Trantos quickly attempted to shake some of them.

"Reech! Reech! Wake up man!" Trantos picked him up in a fireman's carry and loped with the cotton-haired-joe tossed right over his shoulder. Unfortunately, it wasn't going to work; the dead weight proved to be too much for the swordsman. Trantos was not equipped to carry heavy burdens. He began to trip in the sand, and then inevitably he dumped the snoozing old curmudgeon on his head. Trantos could almost feel the great idol's shadow fall on him. He whirled about from his prone position in the sand and saw a terrifying vision.

The giant stood upon two pillar-like legs and towered over the jungle like a high-rise building. Its entire form, from head to toe, was made up of hundreds of man-shaped nuggets, most of them in awful, shrieking poses, frozen, welded forever into the very body of the giant.

"No!" Trantos said as he back-pedaled away from the walking monolith, barely evading capture when it closed in and instead scooped up Reech into its gargantuan golden hand.

On the south side of the pool, where the captain was still attempting to awaken more men, he witnessed the behemoth lurch down and pick Reech up from the sand. *"Noooo, not my navigator!"*

He looked around at his own half of the crew for help, but they too had indulged in the purple bananas, and began to drift off.

"Don't eat the bananas," Kastos yelled as he ran through them. "They are enchanted!"

The bracelet tied to his scabbard began to hum, and another message from Keisha entered his mind.

Kastos you must come back to the ship ... there is trouble.

Kastos wanted to do just that, but he had enough problems at the moment. He looked in awe at the tremendous walking statue as it lifted Reech high into the air and then merged the chart reader into its rotund torso. Reech had been sleeping when the gold man had grasped him, but awoke dangling in mid-air, screaming in terror. Then the navigator was mashed and frozen into the great, golden belly of the statue, fused right in along with the other man-shaped nuggets.

The other crewmembers suffered the same fate and joined the giant's anatomy—plucked from a nap, and melted into its form, where they became one with the metal.

Kastos waved at Trantos in an attempt to draw his attention.

"Over here man, quickly, we have to go back to the boat."

Trantos spotted the captain and veered off towards him. He outmaneuvered the lumbering colossus who was hardly as dexterous. Still, the great thing pivoted on one enormous foot, like a slow basketball player, and began trudging in their direction.

The sole surviving duo of the land-bound crew, Kastos and Trantos, ran for their very lives. Each one half expected the gigantic hand to snatch them up at any second. Yet, soon they had out distanced the behemoth, much to their relief.

At the moment it felt safe enough for Kastos to look over his shoulder, he saw that the pursuer was blocked by some trees. However, it would only be a matter of a few minutes before the coconut palms were pushed down and cleared by the behemoth's carven, sandaled foot.

"Follow me, Trantos, we must hurry!"

They ran like madmen, at a speed that neither of them thought that they owned. They both narrowly escaped capture by the giant and barely made it out to where the boats were.

Only the boats were not there.

Neither was Hairybear.

The gold giant tromped through the last of the jungle and entered the lagoon clearing where the two men stood by the water's edge.

"We have to swim for the boat." Trantos suggested.

It was true, yet Kastos could only stare in stunned disbelief at the spot where the missing skiffs were supposed to be.

Another moment later and they were entering the warm, blue-green waters of the small inlet and swimming as if they were Olympic athletes, towards the lagoon opening where the *Kella* stood anchored offshore.

"We will never make it!" Trantos wailed through a mouthful of water as he swam. The ship was yards away and the colossus had entered the shallow water behind them. Soon the cumbersome form would be on top of them, as it could stride much faster than they could stroke.

"I think we are done for, Trantos," even Kantos himself had to admit.

Then out of nowhere came a long, cylindrical tank, flying end over end through the air and hitting the nugget-encrusted behemoth directly on its huge, jug-shaped head. Instantly a great cloud of white, billowing frost seemed to envelop the gold giant, and then settled, congruent to a great film of dust. Yet, this was no mere sprinkling of powder, this was some unknown chemical that was contained within the cylinder that Hairybear had found.

As if the gold giant suspected the danger it attempted to fall back, yet it was far too late, and the giant began to freeze. Then it started to crack and fall apart into pieces. Large chunks of it slid from its mountainous bulk and splashed into the blue-green waters of the lagoon. Moments later, the guardian of the island had been reduced into a pile of steaming rubble. Yet, the two men were not out of danger. They still floundered helplessly in the water, and this time it was against a spreading pool of the white, vaporous fluid that exploded from the cylinder. The vapor surrounded the huge, frozen boulders that were all that remained of the giant, rippling outward in all directions, killing everything swimming in its proximity—fish, eel and crab—and soon it would touch the two men. It was only a matter of seconds, and they too would suffer the same fate as the gold golem.

Then out of nowhere came eight pairs of hands pulling them out of the tainted lagoon. They had been saved at the very last second. By the smell of the fishy arms and hands that had appeared to assist them, it was obvious that Keisha's fellow fish-men had come to their rescue. Kastos looked up in exhaustion at them as he lay on the deck of the small craft. His heart was heavy with the loss of his crew, yet he was grateful all the same that these deep ones were taking them away from the bubbling destruction that was once a placid, tropical lagoon.

9

Once back on board the ship, the message Keisha had sent about trouble on the ship came clear to Kastos. Hairybear and a small group of his sympathizing crewmembers had taken over the bridge while everyone was being slaughtered by the giant. The mutiny he led was supported by the fact that he had the technological insight as to what the weapon flung from the catapult would do to the colossus.

"Liquid nitrogen," Hairybear boasted, as he stood there leveling a gun at Kastos and Trantos as they stood dripping wet on the poop deck. It'll freeze anything … something that you assholes wouldn't understand unless you were a snipe like me."

Kastos stood tall, regardless of the fact that several rifles were pointed at him. Even though the captain was at the disadvantage, he acted nonetheless with authority.

"You'll never get away with this," he said. Then looked around and saw that the fish-men were also being held at gunpoint and forced to do Hairybear's bidding. Apparently he was expecting to set underway using them as his crew. The sound of a whiplash cracked as one of the mutineers ordered them about. The Fathomers looked none too happy about being made to labor beneath the hot sun, their scaled skin taking on a pinched, shriveled appearance from being made to dry in the heat.

Two of Hairybear's henchmen dragged Keisha over to where Kastos and Trantos were detained. Then they threw her down onto the deck in front of them.

"Hey, that's no way to treat a lady!" Trantos reprimanded.

Hairybear reached out and cracked Trantos across the face with the butt of his rifle. The dandy went down like a sack of grain. Blood ran down from his cheek where he had been struck. He wiped it on the back of his hand and then reached for the hilt of his sword.

"Don't even try it asshole." Hairybear pointed the gun at him and then bade his men to take Trantos' weapon and bind him. Then Hairybear kicked him in the back. Trantos let out a painful bark.

"That's for Turkeyneck, you son-of-a-bitch."

"Enough," Keisha ordered, "you have what you want." Kastos saw that her bracelet had been taken. It was on Hairybear's arm now. He had stolen it for himself.

"Not quite everything." The hull tech pointed at the other bracelet that Kastos had hanging on his belt, ripped it off and then clasped it on his other arm. Kastos was outraged over this outright confiscation, but made no move. He thought that he saw the ghost of a smile on Keisha's lips, and suspected that she knew something about the bracelet that would help them. He gave her the briefest nod that he understood to play dumb and not give away the chance to turn the tables.

"Take them to the brig!" Hairybear ordered. "But bring the bitch up to my stateroom."

"Do we have a brig?" Scag, one of Hairybear's mutineers asked.

"Fucking make one asshole, use the aft winch room."

"Aye, Captain," the gangly sailor said.

"Captain now, eh?" Kastos remarked to the hull tech.

Hairybear ignored him. Instead he ordered his men to tie up everyone and bring them below to the winch room. Trantos remained silent as he watched Hairybear's group as they marveled over his sword and lay claims over who would be the one to possess it. Trantos swore that he would be sure that they would be the first to own it by its business end if he ever managed to escape his fetters.

In the winch room, Kastos sat against the wall, depressed now over the fact that his crew was gone. Also it didn't help matters that Hairybear had taken Keisha to his quarters. Kastos' face held a sullen look that even Trantos could not help but notice, even though his own countenance hurt like hell and resembled a grapefruit from the swelling.

"Kastos, it is not your fault that the men fell sway to the magic of those purple bananas." Trantos murmured. "The place was a trap, we ourselves are lucky to be alive."

It may have been so, but it was small compensation at the moment to Kastos, who could not lift his mood, no matter how he tried. So he attempted to try some sleep since they were tied up like shrimp ready to be fried.

The boat had been rocking because Sharkbait was at the wheel, so it was difficult to rest, yet at long last Kastos finally managed to gain some fitful shut eye, only to be awakened by the sound of footsteps, and keys jingling.

"Someone is coming," Kastos whispered. "Trantos, wake up."

The outer hatch to the winch room had been padlocked on the outside, securing the two prisoners inside. It was a windowless compartment lighted by red lamps alone, so that when the door opened only a small, black shape was visible. Once Kastos and Trantos could focus their eyes they could make out the shining, creamy, black skin and short corn rows of pygmy hair.

"GANK?"

Sure enough, it was the signal-shack hermit himself. Somehow he had managed to gain his place back on board and find a way to reach them. The small, loyal sailor immediately sliced the bonds that restrained both men.

"C'mon, Keisha wants to see you up on the bridge."

"What? How did you ...?" Kastos could only utter.

Gank smiled as he threw aside the severed slices of rope.

"I don't know, all I remember is running like hell through the jungle when that gold giant was chasing me, and then I slipped and fell into a small channel leading into the sea. I hid beneath the water bushes as the thing stomped around. I was shaking like a leaf, so I jumped into the water and swam underwater downstream out into the open sea and grabbed one of the bumper lines dragging off the *Kella*'s railing. After a fucking hour I finally made it on board. I was tired as hell and I heard the giant collapse, and then the mutiny going down. I was too beat to help, so I crawled into a boatswain's locker until I gained my strength and came up with a plan to help."

Trantos patted the man on the back.

"Well, I guess you must have come up with a master plan, my friend!"

Gank shook his head: "No, it wasn't me. I was awoken by the sound of queer screaming coming from up on the bridge, and then, after mustering the nerve to go look, I saw that there were strange, colorful lights also coming from there. There was no sign of the men who were with Hairybear, the ones who helped with the mutiny. Not at first anyway, but once I saw the trail of blood, I discovered what had happened to them."

Kastos raised an eyebrow, Gank had piqued his interest.

"Well, go on … what happened to them?"

"They had been eaten, sir. The fish-men had somehow gotten the better of them and were eating them for dinner on the poop deck, alive. The screams and gore were horrific."

"Good." Trantos grinned.

"Yeah," Gank agreed, "save for the fact that my fat little ass might have been also chewed up, but they let me walk right through them. One of them pointed up to the bridge and I saw Keisha standing there looking down at me. She waved me up, and that's when I saw what had happened to Hairybear—he had turned into a *merman! Like one of the Fathomers!*"

Chills went up and down Kastos' spine as he heard this.

"I went up to the bridge and flopping around on the floor was a big, tuna of a thing with long, squid-like flipper arms. Part of his hull technician uniform was still on his bloated body and those two strange bracelets of hers were clasped on his tubular arms. In a terrible, guttural voice that will haunt me until the day I die I heard Hairybear screaming out of a half-human head that was already turning into a mutated sea-bass. He said, *TAKE THEM OFF! TAKE THE BRACELETS OFF ME!* until nothing else could be understood. Then he stopped fighting it, and seemingly accepted his fate. That's when the bracelets suddenly opened and fell from his paddle arms, as if with a life all their own."

Kastos nodded. He knew that the bracelets did have a life all their own, and although he was grateful for the mutiny being over, and he and Trantos free, he still had reservations about Keisha, the bracelets and what effect it all might have on his ultimate quest.

The feel of the sea beneath his ship was different.

"I'm going to see her." He strode ahead of them through the passageway, with a sense of haste. The feeling that time was growing short became overwhelmingly intense.

10

Once on the bridge, Kastos could well see that the sky was a deeper, purple color, because they were nearing the southern pole of this wasted world. The wind took on a sharp, colder edge that made them want to cover up with heavy, foul-weather jackets.

The Fathomers, however, were undaunted by the frigid weather. In fact, they even seemed to like it.

Keisha stood against the view screen of the ship with the great dome of the sky as her backdrop. To Kastos she appeared almost primal, as if she were not human, just an animal inside of a human shell. Her eyes were feral, almost hostile. Kastos decided to tread carefully around her, not wanting to become vexed, or worse.

"I can't thank you enough for your help," Kastos offered, then held his arms out to the wild-looking female.

"We will continue on our journey to the shore of the old gods now," Keisha said.

Kastos looked at the compass. The ship was drifting on uncharted waters.

"How are we supposed to get there now without a crew?" Kastos said, giving her a baleful glance. "And without a navigator, how shall we even find it? Reech is gone."

"Take these," she said, holding out the bracelets towards him, "with these the ship will obey your every command."

Kastos wondered if this was a trick, if he would turn into a fish-man if he accepted them, but intuition told him that it was right for him to have them. So, without hesitating, he clasped them on to both of his arms, for better or worse.

The compass on the ship started to spin, and then amazingly, the inert dials and lights on the consoles began to light up, matching the color of the twin suns that were very small and distant on this southern horizon.

Kastos was amazed to find that he could move the ship at will, and he also heard the voice of Reech speaking in his head, telling him the coordinates to Atacania, where the fortress of the old gods awaited.

Use the bracelets to their full capacity. They will take you to your destiny.

Kastos felt his arms fill with gooseflesh at the sound of the old curmudgeon's voice, understanding that even death itself would not stand in the way of his quest.

As the *Kella* sailed further into the waters of the southern pole, the sky began to turn black. The dancing light of the tandem suns did not reach this far south. The waters gave off an eerie phosphorous glow that Kastos would call *corpse light*. Thirty leagues below the surface, in the deepest depths, explosions that resembled underwater fireworks filled the darkness. The Fathomers became all worked up about the silent blossoms of those brilliant flashes, abandoning their angling and whatever else remained of the mutineers' gristle-filled bones as they congregated by the railing. A murmur arose among them and they pointed down into the spectacle-filled waters, their watery gullets voicing out their garbled speech that nobody understood except for Keisha.

"What are they saying?" Kastos asked.

"They speak of their ancestors calling to them from the crevices in the ocean floor, telling them to leap overboard and join them, lest doom befall them. Their race is forbidden to set fin upon dry land, never mind the shores of the old gods."

"Everyone is forbidden to go there!" Gank added, his fat little brown pygmy face sweating despite the now chilly climate. Trantos showed up behind them, having recovered his sword. He gazed down at one of the Fathomers, a rather large one, who stood by the other fish-men.

"Is that … Hairybear?"

Surely it was. In fact he still wore the hull technician uniform that he prided himself so much on, although it had been nearly ripped to shreds by the transformation.

"Yeah that's him," Kastos observed, "Wow ... just when you think you've seen it all."

"True, nevertheless, the Fathomers will follow the laws of nature although *all* of them had once been subject to the change brought on by the bracelets, your enemy Hairybear included." Keisha explained. "It would be best to let them depart, lest they become violent. They outnumber us greatly."

Trantos whipped out his long blade, which flashed in the light of the floating blowfish lanterns.

"Let them try, for they will find Trantos to be a fit enough swordsman to die by."

Kastos sensed the repulsion and the contempt that the dandy held for the fish-men from when he saw them eating human flesh. He was ready to leap at them and cut them to pieces.

"No, Trantos," Kastos said, staying him from starting a battle that could only end badly. "I think that we shall let them go in peace. We don't need them for the remainder of this journey."

One by one the deep ones lined up and hurled themselves overboard. Once they hit the water their merman bodies transformed into a form even more suitable for aquatic travel. Their spines extended out into long, flat tails and their legs disappeared altogether. Only the forearms remained, turning into long, paddle-shaped flippers. It was a reversal of the evolutionary process.

The remaining crew of the *Kella* watched in astonishment as the morphing silhouettes swam against the silent, exploding blooms of color that erupted beneath them. They went deeper and deeper until they vanished from sight. Then the mysterious fathomers were gone.

The cold air began to distract Kastos and company, the polar darkness was ahead of them, and it was time to go below decks and prepare for the night.

The coal furnace that fueled the ship provided enough warmth for the compartments nearest to the bridge, and since the ship was piloted now by thaumaturgical means there was no need to man any of the stations. The crew could take some rest before the last leg of their voyage.

Kastos was not surprised to see that Keisha wanted to sleep by herself. It was symptomatic of her frosty attitude towards him since that night the bracelets had fallen from her arms, when he had the dream where she asked him to make a choice.

Before he went to sleep in his captain's quarters alone, he stood outside and gazed up at the black, starless sky that marked the bottom of the world. Not even the broken-toothed face of the moon would reveal itself to this place. This was truly the pit of the planet. After some time, he worked himself up to pay a visit to Keisha where she slept. She had chosen the crew's lounge. The door was unlocked so he crept in. In the dim globe of the rockfish lantern he leaned over to kiss her cheek goodnight.

There was a small mark on her face that Kastos did not like. It looked like a sore, and reminded him of the pox that she was covered with in the dream when he proclaimed his decision to *choose her.*

No matter, he did not want to awaken her. She probably had her own reasons for sleeping alone. He shrugged his shoulders and returned to his stateroom and went to bed, exhausted from the entire ordeal.

Kastos tossed and turned as nightmares filled his head.

It was difficult for him to determine whether he was dreaming or not. The constant creaking of the ship in these strange waters kept him in a state of half-sleep that trapped him between two realms. There was also a voice that droned in his head proclaiming to be the very face of the waters protesting against his ship's trespass. Fear tried to fill the wanderer's heart and he found himself warding off the taunts by exhibiting the sign of the mortal coil. He tried to swim up out of the murk, but to no avail—he was along for the ride. Some force was pulling him down into darkness. He fell through a black hole seemingly torn out of the veil of reality, a curtain that had been cast up to hide the realm of the ancient ones. Then he saw a mountain of black stone towers sticking out of the ice, the ramparts of Xoth itself, the fortress of the old gods.

There he beheld horrors locked within shielded chambers that were shrieking in seemingly pain-filled madness. There was the cell of Sgurd, the chamber of the Zogg Glyptus, and the dungeon of Syryops. Syryops was the one Keisha called the gatekeeper, whom Kastos must face in order to fulfill his destiny. All of these terrible entities had been banished here after the fall of the old father. Waiting for the day when the proper star configurations finally allowed them to rotate back into the world, the ancient ones were condemned here at the icy wastes of Atacania, where the secret portal supposedly existed.

In this dream Kastos found himself flying through the frozen night towards those black towers, and then into a yawning tunnel that bored into the base of the mountain. Into that lightless hole he flew, and once inside he was attacked by horror after horror.

Kastos felt nothing less than revulsion over the sight and feel of those mutated invertebrates with partial human anatomy. These were the hordes that awaited him in the bowels of Atacania.

And the glowing green strands that he had seen before when—

When he had dreamed of Keisha, when he had promised that he would choose her, but why?

He awoke abruptly when the ship took a violent lurch. Trantos was yelling, which also brought Kastos up from his wretched sleep. It felt as if the sea had risen and tossed the *Kella* about like a cork in a storm.

"It's a tsunami," Trantos explained, "caused by the underwater volcanic activity we saw when the fish-men swam down into the depths. *We are caught upon a giant wave!*"

Kastos jumped from his rack and compelled his will into the golden bracelets that he wore and mentally labored to commandeer the ship. It was as if the ocean itself was rejecting his boat from the waters of the immortals. Only the power of the bracelets kept them from being sucked down. Trantos took a chance and stuck his head topside through a hatch and spotted a dreadful-looking shoreline that was dead ahead. Towering black pinnacles of stone jutted up towards an eerie, green sky that was filled with oppressive clouds. Here was the forbidden continent of Atacania, where sat the kingdom of Xoth.

It was the place of exile prepared for the old gods who were banished long ago.

"We're gonna crash, man!" Trantos screamed, almost having a spasm. He jumped back down the ladder and slammed the hatch shut. *"There is a very rocky land mass dead ahead!"*

It was time to make for the bridge.

Kastos knew that they were about to scuttle upon the shores of Xoth unless he put all of his powers of meditation into *lifting* the boat with the power of the bracelets. The wristlets had the ability within them, but it would be up to Kastos' concentrated efforts to pull it off.

After the captain reached the bridge, he stood with each foot squarely placed on the floor in an assault position, focusing through the view screen at the point of impact that was soon to arrive.

The bracelets glowed with hidden fire, and then with a tremendous psychic heave Kastos *tipped* the bow of the *Kella* upward, so that it rode on top of the wave like a great surfboard. It missed the sharp teeth of the broken pylons and skidded over the top of the cliff that was even with the height of the tidal wave. Then the *Kella* was thrown onto the rugged land, similar to a paper airplane being tossed from a child's hand. It was bashed, and battered, but eventually the colorfully painted frigate came to rest with a groaning screech atop a craggy arm of basalt. Although it rocked precariously off balance, the *Kella* finally settled on a forty-five-degree angle with the bow pointed straight up towards the shadow haunted fortress of Xoth.

Kastos exhaled with relief, his long hair wrapped around his face like a tattered banner. He looked down and saw that the fire of his bracelets had gone dormant. Then he turned his head and beheld the hellish gates of the black city before him.

11

It lay across a field of ice filled with cracks and pits where wisps of poisonous vapor and clouds of deadly gas emerged. Giant, rusted culverts constructed out of slag iron dumped chemicals and toxins manufactured from the endless amount of nightmarish foundries and factories stretching out below the towers. Clouds of freezing black snow blew across these plains of despair, from a howling wind that uncovered the twisted, deformed shapes of creatures that were best not described. Fortunately for Kastos and crew all of these sick things were frozen solid. A single lone road led through this nightscape towards the entrance of Xoth.

"Unnnnhhh."

Kastos heard the sound behind him, then turned and saw that poor Gank had been impaled upon a sheared angle-iron during the crash. He dangled from it like a caught pogie. The steel had punctured one of his lungs. Blood sputtered out of his mouth, down his chin and onto his chest when he tried to talk.

"FUCK," Trantos cried. Then he and Kastos immediately set to pulling Gank free. A torturous, painful, affair, but Gank never uttered a single cry. Wherever pygmies like him came from, they sure knew how to make them tough.

They lay him down on the deck. His face was turning darker, and he was fading.

"He's got a sucking chest wound," Trantos said. "We gotta save him ... grab a piece of plastic ... an I.D. card or something!"

"Trantos ... "

"Listen, I think it's closing up, I got it covered with my hand."

"Trantos ... he's gone."

It was true, Gank had gone to pygmy heaven. He had much more than a leak in his lung, it was shorn through with a four-by-six-inch hole that you could stick your fist through. Trantos knew it. He took off his hat and bowed his head, then wiped snot from his nose and returned his cover.

"This sucks ... he was a good little guy."

When it suddenly occurred to Kastos that they had not yet accounted for Keisha, he was filled with alarm. He left Trantos to mourn Gank alone and ran towards her cabin, knocking wreckage, sparking cables and pieces of broken bulkhead out of his way as he did so.

This time he did not bother being quiet, but wrenched open her door. It was blocked by old benches and other lounge furniture that had fallen about during the crash. He pushed harder and then he was standing inside, looking at her as she lay on the largest of the old couches, facing the wall, with a blanket pulled over her head. Hopefully she was just sleeping, although it was not likely.

"Keisha?"

No answer.

He gently shook her shoulder, and the covering fell from her. He was shocked by the sight of her hair. It had turned completely gray, some of it even missing in patches. Her skin was a black, wrinkled parchment akin to that of a mummy from far-off Aegypt. She was dead, as if for ages, so dried up that her skin began to flake off from the exposure to the air. He could not bear to turn her around and look at her face. He wanted to remember her the way she was when she was alive. Tenderly he placed the blanket back over her head, and then kissed her on the place where her lips lay beneath it.

Choose me Kastos, choose me ... and I will love you forever.

The words rang in his head like the tolling of a big, black funeral bell.

Trantos came to find Kastos sitting on the bridge. He was gearing up for the infiltration of Xoth. There was a pile of foul-weather clothing to pick through. He also found a large, rusty, machete-style sword for Kastos to use. That would have to suffice since they had no guns. The fathomers had taken the guns and thrown them overboard after eating the mutineers. It did not matter because Trantos did not think that this battle could be won with such weapons. He believed that the bracelets were the key to winning the fight.

"Are we going to cross that plain, are we going into that hell hole?" Trantos asked, his face was heated with an evil smile. He wanted payback for Gank.

"Yes … but I cannot guarantee a return trip. You must decide for yourself if you want to follow me to my doom. Maybe you could take your chances setting out in a lifeboat made into a skiff. As you can see, the ocean has settled down."

It was true, but Trantos shook his head as he looked out at the placid, steel-colored waters. It would be a long journey, with no idea of where he was going, and anyway, he had no intention of leaving a good fight.

"No, my Captain, this is a one-way journey for me as well, I shall follow you until the wheel of fortune that turns the universe decides otherwise. Besides, you might have need of my swift sword hand soon."

The two men set out from the ship, climbing down with ropes from the rock upon which it was perched, and touched down on the dirty ice of Atacania.

"The ice has veins of crimson within it. I can see red blotches in it that remind me of the butcher's window back in Idylldale."

"It's blood, from all of the dead things that are under it, slain back when this place was taken over by the old gods."

"Why aren't the bracelets working?" Trantos asked.

"I don't know. I can't get them to do anything since we crashed."

"That is not good."

As they walked on the lone road over this massive plain of frozen monsters they came upon the vent holes. Steam emitted that would melt the frozen, bloody ice nearest the holes to a gore-filled slush. Their nostrils filled with a stench beyond belief that was so bad it made them vomit. Nevertheless, Kastos and Trantos were grateful for those vent holes to warm up their cold bodies. The wind gusts and snow squalls were intense, yet still they trudged on. Two small figures moving slowly towards the deadly fortress city, but there was still no sign of any of the inhabitants. The silence of Xoth was, eerily, too quiet. Kastos wondered if they were walking into an ambush.

Once they were they in the shadow of those morbid towers the sound of sirens began to wail with a soul-chilling, nightmare whine. Then heavy machinery thrummed into life underneath the ground as the great vaults opened to release the nightmare hordes.

"Quickly, over here." Trantos had spotted a sewer pipe that was sticking out from beneath the base of the mountain. A place where they could hide just before the enemy emerged.

So quickly, and stealthily, under cover of the shadow cast by the walls, they left the road, and ran over the slush-filled, corpse-filled mud towards the pipe. Gigantic crab shapes and other monstrous invertebrates had died out here, frozen into the mud, probably enslaved denizens of the sea that had been ensnared and twisted into these shapes by Syryops.

He had been bred by the old gods, altered with dark, cruel arts, and then raised on the blood of countless poor mortals who had been unfortunate enough to be captured.

Now the air began to shimmer from the gases expelled from the pits, filled with nightmare inducing delusions.

The masters of this realm began to send out wave after wave of illusions. The visions barraged the men. There were terrifying walls of fire that turned into demonic faces, or tall, spidery horrors with eyes that expanded to the size of hot air balloons. Next, a tidal wave of blood, filled with mutated sharks and many-tentacled devil fish that had mouths containing long, surrealistic needle teeth dripping deadly venom.

Kastos held firm in spite of these sensory onslaughts, realizing that this was not a physical attack, but the gas merely playing on their minds.

"Don't let these light shows deter us," Kastos smiled, "these are only false illusions sent out to demoralize us. The real fight still waits."

At last they reached the safety of the small culvert, just as more horrific images took the stage. And even though they were not real, Trantos did not want to witness any more of the visions.

Finally the strange siren calls ceased and the gas illusions dispersed, the first line of defense having been broken. Kastos and Trantos sat tight, and after a very tense silence a loud horn blasted. Next, a thunderous roar followed, which was the war cry of an army who serve as the guard. They poured out of Xoth in a steady stream, meaning to search and destroy, a rioting flood of thrashing, malformed horrors. Half-sea creature half-human, reminding Kastos of what Hairybear had become. Kastos thought it was evident why the great field was layered with the remains of so many creatures, because it was *these* that were constantly sent out from the gates to do the fighting, and then simply left to freeze and die on the ice.

Kastos and Trantos had no choice but to engage in fighting, there were simply too many of them. Kastos and Trantos had to abandon the pipe before becoming trapped inside of its dead end.

The two men fought against these denizens of damnation for many hours, and they still did not make a dent. More kept right on coming. Dead squid-men were piled up all around them; both Kastos and Trantos were covered in the slick, putrid, black blood of the things.

Trantos looked over at the gates. It appeared as if the enemy forces were finally beginning to abate. There might be an opportunity for Kastos to enter and fulfill his quest. The swordsman pushed the captain towards it, and then stood between him and another onrushing mob of horrors.

"Hurry while I hold them back," Trantos said. "The front gate is clear."

"What? Are you serious?" Kastos yelled, as his sword lopped off heads and tentacles alike. The squid-men had no weapons; they fought with their beaks, tentacles and stinging suckers. They pulled you into them, so that they could try to rip out your throat.

"Yes," Trantos answered, taking out three enemies with three lightning quick thrusts. "You must go in and fulfill your destiny. Take those bracelets into that city and try to do whatever the fuck you're supposed to do with them."

Kastos was still hesitant. He did not want to abandon his comrade to certain death.

"This is my call, Captain. Fare thee well."

Trantos turned and threw himself at the enemy. "For Reech! For Gank!" he cried as his sword flashed into life with the alacrity of a metal musician from back in the ancient times. His face grinned like a demon as he hacked and slashed and covered the ground with their flesh, adding them to the thousands of cousins waiting to greet them in the frozen multileveled layers of ice.

It was time for Kastos to head for the inner sanctum of Xoth. He felt the bracelets coming alive again, vibrating as they did when they began to power up.

Before Kastos moved into the gigantic front doorway to Xoth, he turned back one last time and looked at Trantos. His final sight of him was only a sword that flashed in the dark, so fast that it was only a blur that chopped off snout and limb. Trantos made a blood fog that hung around him and cloaked him in its crimson haze. Kastos knew that it was a matter of time before the swordsman was overwhelmed. Too many of the things had been drawn to him from the gates, and there were more that came up from the maggot holes in the fields. Kastos saluted and then entered Xoth's crudely sculpted entranceway before another wave of the nightmare race came pouring out of it and blocked his way.

12

Kastos came upon a few straggling creatures inside of the huge black corridor that were more of a nuisance than any real danger. So he dispatched them quickly and quietly with his own crude machete.

The upcoming battle with the gatekeeper was going to prove to be the real challenge. Kastos judged by the corpse-like, green, dim glow that emanated from the end of the tunnel's inky darkness that he was approaching the inner sanctum. A short time later and the tunnel opened out and brought Kastos into a vast cavern with walls of black onyx. The corridor that brought him here turned into a walkway that ended abruptly, with no ending platform, directly over a pit of unearthly green lava. The great open chamber had columns of veined marble and archways that were finely carven out of the very stone walls, although at present they appeared crumbled and ruined with time. This elegant architecture had been left behind by a once wiser and kinder culture long forgotten even before the old gods were sent here in exile. Years of their defilement had ruined the great work that had once been done here.

A great terrace had been built upon the far side of the great well, and it was filled with robed priests of the unspeakable thing that resided below. They watched Kastos as he stepped up to the end of the causeway. They hissed maliciously. the threw a volley of spells at him, meaning to turn the trespasser away. However, Kastos was prepared, and the bracelets were glowing with a fierce amber fire that turned the hideous, hybrid, squid-priests back into their rat holes. He held the creatures high over his head and allowed the bright shining beams of light to strike them as they shrieked and fled, causing them to suffer pinhole burns from the power of the light that was within them.

Kastos looked down into to the pit. Its green glow bathed him, giving him his own corpse-like cast. He saw a primordial soup filled with enormous chunks that could only be described as flesh, tissue, organs, and the wet bones of a titan. Winding around this brimming stew of gore was something that resembled a colossal spinal column, or maybe it was a tail, Kastos was not certain. It was the size of a train.

Bobbing around in the plasmatic mess were seven eyeballs; each one of them moved with with a life of its own. Some of the eyeballs were lidded, and they widened as they stared up at Kastos and became aware of him.

This is Syryops, Kastos thought, *the gatekeeper.*

Kastos wanted to scream as he felt the god enter his head and try to make him take off the magic bracelets. Syryops wanted Kastos to hurl himself naked into the boiling cauldron below and become a part of the gatekeeper's unformed glory. Kastos trembled and as he used all of his will to resist, he could feel a trickle of blood exit his nostril from the exerted pressure of his meditation.

Syryops sensed this and pushed more.

Kastos' mind was bombarded with every negative thing that had ever happened to him in his life. He saw his parents eaten alive by smegs when he was a boy, how he had barely escaped alive himself to scratch a living off a land that was filled with mutants and monsters. He saw his wife raped and murdered by the barbaric sadists who had kidnapped them both, and made him watch, until he freed himself and exacted a terrible revenge. It didn't help bring her back. It didn't even bring him the satisfaction that he thought it would. He witnessed again everyone he ever loved being taken from him by diseases and death. The visions made him sick, made him tired, made him weak.

Then the thing in the pit began to talk to him in a terrible, booming voice that nearly ripped his head apart.

"So, lowly mortal, you have found your way to the cage of my keeping. It may be only a matter of time before others as base as yourself follow. Others who will seek to find out the secrets that can unlock

eternity, which only the gods themselves are allowed to know.

"Not since the end of the age of the forgotten ones have I spoken with such insignificant beings as you. Not since the very first world was nothing more than an amniotic pool of liquid light. Gaze upon my greatness, base mortal being ... gaze upon me before you dieeeee."

The churning horror within the pit began to rise up to a towering height of over three hundred feet, rearing high against the cavernous walls. Then it leered over Kastos, appearing as a glowing, inside-out corpse that dripped a sizzling, green acid. Titanic ribs were exposed that contained squirming, writhing shapes within that were that were either more squid creatures or innards. This was topped off by a hideously oval-shaped head. It had no face. It was featureless save for seven eyes that roamed every which way; they reminded Kastos of rolling marbles. The parts of it that did have flesh appeared horribly mottled and covered in blue-black blotches. It had two pillar-sized arms mounted onto its terrible frame tapering off into eel-shaped lengths. These Goliath-sized appendages lashed out and shattered the cavernous walls. The heavy limbs of the god caused boulders to fall on the underlings who still lurked boldly about on the balustrade.

Tremors filled the cave and then Kastos lost his balance, toppling forward and into the pit.

The high adventurer was abruptly caught in one of those massive whips. It encircled his waist with a burning, stinging sensation and then he was brought up to Syryops' terrible face. The titan's countenance opened vertically and exhibited a slitted mouth filled with rows of lamprey teeth, along with poisonous green strands that wriggled out from its deep gullet and went for the captain's throat.

Kastos was close enough to feel the hot, fetid oven of its breath on his face. It smelled like a lake of dead bodies, which indeed is what it really was. Another second later and he would be dissolved into the thing by way of those bizarre tendrils that reached out to grasp him.

"NO YOU WILL NOT DO THIS!"

The voice came from above. Kastos turned his head and saw the golden apparition of a lady descend out of the darkness of the vaulted ceiling. She was filled with a blazing light that was as brilliant as a star. Kastos looked upon her dazzling countenance and recognized her instantly.

It was Keisha.

Or maybe it was her spirit.

Kastos watched her float down out of the black, a ghost from the beyond, with white rays of light that pierced the divine flesh of the gatekeeper and caused it to roar in pain.

As ulcerations spread all over its piebald form, Syryops screamed in anguish. Kastos' bracelets began to emit lasers that burned away at the old god as well. Searing the incomplete god with the very light that it had chosen never to behold again.

Brighter and brighter the floating phantom of Keisha shone, blinding the beast. It began to open its mouth wider into an abyss filled with the reek of its insides.

Kastos managed to wiggle his sword arm free.

Without warning Syryops spat a volley of green strands at the spirit form of Keisha, enwrapped her in the coils and commencing to negate her power. She began to scream as if she were in mortal agony.

Then the strands pulled her towards the gaping hole of Syryops' mouth, and swallowed her down into its darkness.

"No, Keisha, NOOOOOOO!" Kastos used his free sword arm to hack away at the constricting tentacle and then launched himself straight at the largest of the entity's seven eyes, empowered by the power surging through the glowing bracelets. Then he plunged the tip of the sword right into its biggest, ugliest, most opaque pupil.

What followed next was a resounding explosion that took man, god and apparition alike, and Kastos the high adventurer fell into the black.

When Kastos awoke he was stark naked and lying face down upon a smooth floor. He turned over, sat up and realized that he was in a hallway, seemingly made out of gold. The walls were broken only by small areas of decorative trim that repeated in a pattern to an infinite length. The place was lit from an unseen source that came from behind the paneling, yet it was impossible to see the ceilings. They were invisible to his eye, stretching upward and disappearing into the above darkness. If there was a barrier, then it was too far up in the black for him to see.

Kastos stood up on his bare feet, foggy and confused. He was aware of the fact that he was not sweating, even though he was nervous.

His body did not feel solid enough to perspire. He felt ethereal.

Kastos could not recollect anything about his past. Everything was in shadow. His life was a dream that he could not remember upon awakening.

At the opposite end, the corridor did not go on for eternity, but instead ended in a foyer where a single object stood. It was a life-sized statue of a beautiful, robed woman, wrought of gold. Her arms were accessorized with a pair of ornate gold bracelets that intrigued Kastos.

A feeling of *déjà vu* passed through him, and a phrase came into his head. It was almost as if the gold-cast woman had whispered aloud to him, speaking to him in his thoughts with her own personal message.

Thank you for choosing me Kastos, thank you, I will love you forever.

He stepped around the statue and came before a set of large double doors. They too reached up into the vaulted height so that their tops also disappeared into darkness. There was a single word engraved across them, three letters with the seam running up through the one in the center. It said:

GUF

There were two handles, one on each door, Kastos reached down and pulled both of them open and stepped through. Suddenly he entered a universe of black filled with the pointed lights of trillions of stars.

Kastos was only just a single one of those stars, joining the numerous flitting, laughing beings as he allowed the doors to the gold corridor to close behind him.

Kastos had no knowledge of how long he stayed in the room

of Guf, with the others like himself who had made it through to this ancient, mysterious well where newborn souls choose their own parents. But after some time an aperture opened before him and he was drawn to it. Excitement overwhelmed him, even though the cold, frigid air and the blinding light promised him an uncomfortable arrival to wherever he was going.

Kastos was pulled towards the opening. He had no choice but to go wherever the illumination filling his vision took him.

A great golden light spilled over Kastos, welcoming him into a realm that felt raw, harsh, cold and all too real. He lost the meager sense of self that he had, as this narrow passage expelled him out of the cozy dark of the star-filled void, and into this place of frigid light.

EPILOGUE

The infant came out of the womb of Keisha Kastonoski and at first appeared stillborn. But once the doctors administered the customary whack on the buttocks which cleared the lungs and started it crying, she knew that it was fine.

When the mother and the son were finally resting in their room she enjoyed her first feeding. Outside the window a beautiful sunrise displayed the most spectacular colors that she could remember, filling her with so much emotion that tears struck her eyes. Through the blur of tears, she looked at the beautiful bracelets given back to her to wear after her delivery. The scintillating beams of light made star points that were nothing less than magical to look at.

"I will think I'll call him Kenneth … Kenneth Kastonoski. Doesn't that sound fitting," she said as she watched her little man with the small patch of red baby hair feed. His tiny hands played with his mother's bracelets as they gleamed in the golden rays of the sun.

FIN

ABOUT THE AUTHOR

Don Paresi was born in Middletown, Connecticut on January 17, 1962. After graduating high school he then served in the U.S. Navy where many ideas for his writings were conceived. After settling down into a marriage with two children Don diligently began to pursue his craft. He is known as artist/writer of the *Sepulcher* comic book mini-series and author of the *Shadowplaces Tales* short story collection published by Steve Woron's Illustration Studio, as well as cover art for three of David Niall Wilson's books: *Ancient Eyes, Vintage Soul* and *Defining Moments.* At present Don spends most of his time in the creative environment of his studio working on future projects.

Made in the USA
Las Vegas, NV
20 July 2021

26728275R00056